Sin tossed Cathy a small velvet jeweler's box. Startled, she caught it with one hand.

"Don't look so frightened." He grinned suddenly. "It's not an engagement ring."

"I hadn't thought it was," she said with chilly dignity, wondering for not the first time how he managed to read her mind. Quickly she snapped open the lid. Nestled in the black velvet was a long thin chain with a small clear emerald. "What—what is it?"

Sin moved up close to her, his lean strong body dwarfing hers, and took the box out of her nerveless fingers. "It's a chain for your waist. It's supposed to be worn with a bikini." Suiting action to words, he unclasped the tiny catch and drew it around her. It rested just above her hipbones, the emerald winking up at her.

"Sin," Cathy breathed, mesmerized. "I can't accept this. It's too . . . intimate."

"But, Cathy . . . that's why I bought it. . . ."

Dear Reader,

It is our pleasure to bring you romance novels that go beyond category writing. The settings of **Harlequin American Romance** give a sense of place and culture that is uniquely American, and the characters are warm and believable. The stories are of "today" and have been chosen to give variety within the vast scope of romance fiction.

The controversial issue of battered women is rarely found in a contemporary love story. Anne Stuart brings to page a sensitive rendering of a very timely problem. Cathy is a brave heroine who takes her life into her own hands and, with the help of Sinclair MacDonald, learns that relationships are not always ill-fated.

From the early days of Harlequin, our primary concern has been to bring you novels of the highest quality. **Harlequin American Romance** is no exception. Enjoy!

Vivian Stephens

Vivian Stephens
Editorial Director
Harlequin American Romance
919 Third Avenue,
New York, N.Y. 10022

Chain of Love

ANNE STUART

Harlequin Books

TORONTO • NEW YORK • LONDON
AMSTERDAM • PARIS • SYDNEY • HAMBURG
STOCKHOLM • ATHENS • TOKYO • MILAN

Published November 1983

First printing September 1983

ISBN 0-373-16030-5

Chapter One

It was a dream, a nightmare, that she'd relived too many times. That voice, that awful, slurred voice, yelling at her, screaming at her, tormenting her, before the heavy fists followed, crashing down on her, as she helplessly tried to flinch out of his reach. But she had never been fast enough, even though he was always slowed by liquor when the rages came upon him. He'd catch her as she scrambled for the door, and her cries would go unheeded as he'd hit her, again and again and again.

"Are you all right?"

Cathy Whiteheart turned her attention from the crowded highway to her sister's concerned gaze, and managed to summon up the vestiges of a smile. "Of course," she said, her voice slightly rusty. "Why wouldn't I be?"

"You just groaned," Meg said sharply. "And you're white as a sheet."

"I haven't been outside my apartment all summer," she reminded her. "It's no wonder I'm pale."

"You weren't that pale a few moments ago. Were you thinking about Greg?"

Cathy pushed the sunglasses back, huddling deeper into the soft leather seat of the deep blue Mercedes. "I shouldn't have agreed to come with you," she said, ignoring her sister's question.

"You didn't exactly agree." Meg's voice was caustic. "I simply wouldn't take no for an answer. It's been months since we've seen you, Cathy. We've been worried about you."

"I'll be all right," Cathy replied, but the set expression on her pale, stubborn face was far from reassuring.

"I wish I could believe that," Meg said, equaling her stubbornness as she once more turned her attention toward the highway between Georgetown and Annapolis.

The famed Whiteheart obstinacy was about all they had in common, Cathy thought with a wryness unusual for her nowadays as she turned back to the scenery. No one would ever have taken them for sisters. Much as Meg might envy Cathy her willowy height, the shoulder-length curtain of silver-blond hair, and the large, wide-set green eyes, it was Meg who had been inundated with suitors, surrounded by handsome, friendly, eager young men. Pert, short, dark-haired Meg, with her much lamented tendency to put on weight and her less-than-perfect nose was the acknowledged belle of the Whiteheart clan, while Cathy, with her classic, untouchable looks had led a surprisingly cloistered existence. It wasn't that she had actively disliked men, she thought musingly. Far from it. But no one had, in most of her twenty-six years, been able to arouse her interest, and the most dedicated men had fallen away in the face of her intractable calm. If only it had stayed that way.

But owning and running a day-care center hadn't put her much in the way of eligible men, so that by the time Greg Danville had appeared in her life, with his handsome face, puppy-dog air and absurdly vulnerable demeanor she had fallen hard, too hard. And then had been unable to pull herself out of the quicksand of a suddenly destructive relationship until it was too late, and she was scarred for life, emotionally if not physically. Why hadn't she stayed in her apartment, hidden behind the drapes, instead of out here in the bright, merciless October sunlight that reached behind her large, opaque sunglasses? She wasn't ready to face life again. There were times when she doubted she ever would be.

Meg had kept up an inconsequential flow of chatter, refusing to be discouraged in the face of Cathy's monosyllabic answers. They were almost at the marina when she once more broached the subject that never seemed far from her conversation. "He's not worth it, Cathy."

For a moment Cathy considered not replying. She continued facing out the window, mesmerized by the scenery she had seen many, many times. "Don't you think I know that?" she said finally in a weary, disheartened voice. "I know perfectly well that I was a fool—I never spend a day without realizing it. And I know that my pride was more damaged than my heart. Sometimes I wonder whether I'm capable of falling in love. If I'd loved Greg more maybe I would have put up with less." She sighed bitterly. "I thought he needed me."

"He did, Cathy. But in ways that were no good for either of you, don't you realize that?"

"Of course I realize that. I realize quite a bit," she added, staring out the window with listless eyes. "But then, I haven't had anything to do but sit and think."

"Sometimes I think it's a damned shame Brandon Whiteheart is our father," Meg declared with belated wrath. "It would have done you good to have had to go out and work every day. I still can't imagine why you sold out your share in the day-care center. The work was perfect for you."

"If Brandon Whiteheart wasn't our father, Meg dear," Cathy replied with a trace of her old humor, "and if we each weren't the proud possessors of embarrassingly large trust funds, not to mention all sorts of expectations from Auntie Flo, etcetera, then Greg Danville would have found me less than irresistible, and I wouldn't be in the mess I'm in now."

"If you think he was only after your money, then you haven't looked in the mirror, sweetie."

"I know only too well he was only after my money," Cathy replied wearily. "It was made appallingly clear to me."

Meg, never blessed with a large amount of circumspection, plunged right in. "What exactly did happen? One moment the two of you were all hearts and flowers, engaged to be married, and the next thing I know you've barricaded yourself in a new apartment and Greg had moved in with some politician's daughter."

A shaft of remembered pain shot through Cathy. "Please, Meg. I don't want to think about it."

"But you obviously are. And I think it might help if you talked about it to someone," Meg persisted, her concern and curiosity inextricably entwined.

Cathy knew that nothing but shock tactics would silence her. Turning to face her sister's pert, inquisitive face, she pulled off the enveloping dark glasses that were like a second skin, and her cold, despairing green eyes bored into Meg's startled brown ones. "Do you remember the time I fell off a horse last winter?" she queried calmly enough.

"Of course I do. You were a real mess—two black eyes, a broken rib and a concussion. But what does that—"

"And the time I told you I fell down a flight of stairs?" she continued inexorably.

"Certainly. But why..." Horrified disbelief washed over her face as she swerved over into the opposite lane. She pulled back into her own just in time to avoid an irate Volvo station wagon. "Cathy, I had no idea! How hideous for you! But why didn't you leave him sooner? Why did you let him continue to do that to you?"

"It's very hard to escape from a situation like that," Cathy said wearily, returning her glasses to their customary position on her aquiline nose. "I don't think I could explain, even if I wanted to. Do you suppose we could just drop the subject? Have a nice day sailing, with no bad memories and no broken hearts? Please?" The plea wasn't far removed from tears.

"Of course we can drop it, sweetie," Meg soothed, instantly contrite. "I didn't mean to push. And I'm certain that Charles won't bring it up either. He's always the most tactful of men, my dear husband is, and you can be sure he wouldn't mention something like that in front of a stranger. Not that Sin's a stranger, mind you. We've known him for years—he's one of Charles's very best friends. But you haven't met him yet, so we would hardly be likely to..." Meg's mindless chatter trailed off in the face of Cathy's suddenly wrathful expression.

"Margaret Whiteheart Shannon, if you have dared to fix me up with a blind date I will never,

ever forgive you! At this moment I have no interest in men whatsoever, and if I ever do I will be more than capable of finding my own. I've spent the last three months feeling angry, hurt, and frightened, and I'm not in the mood to have some willowy senator's aide paraded for my inspection. Stop the damned car!''

"He's not a senator's aide, and he's not there for your inspection," Meg said mildly, her face mirroring her guilty conscience. "It's his boat, after all. I couldn't very well tell him he couldn't come along because my sister is afraid of men."

"Damn you, Meg," Cathy said bitterly, determined not to let her see how close to the mark her words had come. "It's not without justification."

"I know it's not," Meg said in a reasonable, sympathetic tone. "I shouldn't have said that. But I'm not trying to fix you up—I can understand you need time. I wish you wouldn't be so suspicious. Charles and I were thinking of buying a boat, and Sin's seemed just the right size."

"So he's a used-boat dealer."

"No, dear. Sin doesn't need our money, and he's very happy with his boat. We're thinking of buying one like it, and he suggested we come along for a day's outing and see if it suited us. As a matter of fact, I expect he'll probably have some sweet young thing along, and you won't have to worry about him making a pass at you. You can sit on deck and glower to your heart's content. Does that make you any happier?" She pulled into a parking lot beside the marina, sliding to a halt with a squealing of tires that years of driving and her husband's exasperation had failed to cure.

"I should never have come," Cathy mumbled.

"Maybe not. But I'm not about to turn around and drive you back to Georgetown. You're here and you're going to enjoy yourself, or so help me I'll throw you overboard as soon as we get out of the harbor." Meg's dark eyes were quite fierce in her heart-shaped face, and there was a pugnacious tilt to her pointed chin; it was a battle of wills. After a moment Cathy laughed—a weak laugh, but it gave Meg hope after she'd all but abandoned it.

"All right," Cathy said, raising her hands in a gesture of defeat. "I'll be good. I'll tap-dance around the deck, flirt with Mr. Whatsisname, keep Charles in stitches . . ."

"His name is Sinclair MacDonald, and he isn't your type at all."

Cathy followed her sister out of the car and down the docks. "And what do you consider my type? Why wouldn't your wonderful Mr. Mac-Donald do?"

"Because Sin is fairly good-looking, intelligent, charming, well-bred, amusing, somewhat danger-ous, and quite, quite kind. Since your only previ-ous lover lacked all those qualities, I'm certain that Sin would never do for a girl with your pecu-liar tastes."

"A great many people have said Greg was

handsome," Cathy said with ill-placed defensiveness.

"His eyes were too close together. And don't go telling me he was charming. I could see through that manufactured bonhomie the moment I saw him. And he certainly wasn't intelligent. If he was, he would never have thrown you over for a round-heels like Susie Daley."

"Could we just possibly stop talking about Greg?" Cathy begged. "I'll make an effort, I promise. I'll even be nice to Mr. Sinclair MacDonald, if you promise me it's not a setup."

"Have I ever set you up before?" Meg demanded, properly incensed.

Despite her overwhelming gloom, Cathy found she had to laugh at her righteous indignation. "Well, there was Charles's assistant at the Division, there was your next-door neighbor." She listed them on her slender, ringless fingers. "There was the young man you took your pottery course with, there was—"

"Enough! I plead guilty. But I know well enough that you're in no mood for matchmaking right now. I have *some* sensitivity, you know," she said, a vague look of guilt hovering around her dark eyes.

"There you are, ladies," Charles's east coast drawl hailed them from up ahead. "We'd just about given up on you."

"Cathy took a bit more persuading than I expected," Meg replied, moving toward the boat with quickening steps. "But I got her here, and that's the main thing. Come along, Cathy," she called back over her shoulder, racing up the gangplank and into her husband's welcoming arms.

Cathy trailed behind, wondering if she could come up with some last-minute excuse. The bright sun, blue sky, and the trim, shining white yacht were all conspiring to bring back the headache that had been her constant companion during the long, sweltering summer months. Desperately she wanted to race back to Georgetown, to her silent apartment with the drawn curtains and the air conditioner, shut away from the fresh sea air and the smiling faces and laughing voices all around her.

She hesitated at the top of the gangplank. "Look, why don't I just catch a bus back to town? I'm not really in the mood for this."

Meg sent her husband a long-suffering look. "You see what I mean? She seems to have developed an allergy to sunshine and fresh air. If you come up with one more complaint, Cathy . . ."

"All right, all right," she acquiesced, giving Charles a kiss on his proffered cheek. "This is a lovely boat, though why you'd need anything quite so large is beyond me."

"It sleeps four. We're planning on using ours to sail down to the Caribbean in the winter like Sin does. Think of the money we'll save in hotel bills!" Meg announced brightly.

"That sounds like your usual idea of wise financial planning," Cathy scoffed. She cast a searching glance about the shiny decks. "Where is our host? Did I scare him away?"

"Sin's gone to pick up some cigarettes. I thought I could do without, but . . ." Charles shrugged.

"And his lady friend?" Cathy inquired in silky tones. Meg was off to one side, making frantic gestures that Charles failed entirely to notice.

"Oh, there's no one else coming. I think Sin's between ladies for the moment. Though he seldom stays that way for long. I've never known anyone with such phenomenal luck with women." Meg's grimaces and signals finally penetrated his abstraction, as did Cathy's motionless stance, her generous mouth compressed in a thin line beneath the large, enveloping sunglasses.

"Oh, you don't need to worry," he added hastily. "I don't think you're Sin's type. He likes them a little more worldly, and a little more rounded, for that matter. You've lost weight this summer," he added bluntly.

"Tactful as ever," Cathy murmured, relaxing her tensed shoulders for the first time that day. It was good to be around Charles and Meg and their tactless concern. She hadn't allowed anyone that close in months.

"No, really, you don't need to worry about Sin. He's absolutely harmless. I'm sure he'll take no more notice of you than if you were a piece of driftwood."

"That bad, am I?" Cathy laughed, the sound rusty from long disuse.

Charles's fair skin flushed. "You know what I mean, Cath. It's just that Sin is . . . well, you know, he's . . ."

"Yes, Charles. What exactly am I?" An amused voice came from directly behind her, though well above her head. With a curious sense of fate, Cathy turned to meet Sinclair MacDonald.

Chapter Two

She had been prepared for height, but not quite the overwhelming size of the man directly behind her. She squinted up at him, way up into the face above her, the mobile mouth, laughing hazel eyes, and she took a hasty step backward, away from all that vibrant masculinity. In her rush of nervousness she tripped, her ankle turning beneath her, and before anyone could move a large, well-shaped hand reached out and caught her elbow, righting her again with just the proper amount of strength and gentleness, and then released her.

"Thank you," she said shakily, the imprint of his hand still burning on the soft, tender skin of her upper arm. Keeping better control of her feet, she backed away, well out of range of that almost overwhelming masculine intensity.

"Sinclair MacDonald, this is my sister-in-law, Cathy Whiteheart. Cath, this is Sin. You've heard me mention him," Charles added with a winning smile that had a nervous edge to it.

"Not that I remember," Cathy said with a stubborn, unencouraging glare at her demure sister. All that potent attraction was having a perverse effect—she was determined to keep this astonishingly attractive man at a distance. There was a look of a sleek, jungle beast about him, for all his affable smile. *Like a panther,* she thought fancifully, edging farther away.

Her host smiled lazily down at her. "Well, you haven't missed anything," he dismissed her rudeness lightly. "Why don't you ladies go below and see if you can rustle up some lunch while Charles and I get under way? It's past noon and I, for one, am starving."

Cathy met the charming grin with stony rage. "Why don't you *gentlemen* fix lunch? Or is that too much like women's work?"

Instead of the anger she expected and hoped for, the amused smile deepened, revealing a disconcerting dimple in one lean, weathered cheek. "A liberated woman?" he inquired smoothly. "I beg your pardon. Why don't Charles and I make lunch, then, while the two of you cast off and get us out of the harbor? You can call us when we've hit open sea." He started toward the cabin.

Cathy's sense of humor, long dormant, surfaced for a brief moment before being engulfed in irritation. "I don't know anything about sailing," she admitted, as her eyes unwillingly took in the length of him.

God, he had a beautiful back! He was wearing a teal blue Ralph Lauren polo shirt stretched across broad, well-muscled shoulders, and the faded jeans that hugged his impossibly long legs looked molded to him. He stopped, turned casually and shrugged. "Well, since I know absolutely nothing about cooking, why don't I take care of the boat and you take care of the food? You can pick your own assistant—I'm sure Charles will be happy to help you if you want to keep everything sexually integrated."

All this was said in such an innocent drawl that Cathy was hard put to control an overwhelming desire to shove his large frame overboard. She wasn't used to verbal sparring, especially with one whose looks were quite distracting, and she suddenly felt the almost desperate need to get away from the hot, bright sun, the blue sky, and the tall, disturbingly handsome man who had already overwhelmed her. She had had enough of being bested by handsome men to last her a lifetime, she thought with a sudden upsurge of self-pity that brought stinging tears to her eyes behind the sunglasses.

Swiftly she headed toward the cabin. "C'mon, Meg," she ordered in a muffled voice.

There was still one problem left to negotiate. Sin MacDonald had stopped in the middle of the narrow passageway to the cabin, his large frame filling the small aisle, and he didn't look as if he was about to move. Cathy moved in on him, determined not to be the first to give way, and he held his ground, the hazel eyes surveying her with lazy amusement as he lounged against the bulkhead. She was forced to stop in front of him, feeling dwarfed, helpless, and frustrated.

The look in her tear-filled eyes was pure hatred. She allowed herself to glare at him, mistakenly thinking the oversized glasses hid her expression. But the anger in the set of her mouth and a stray tear slipping down from beneath the glasses told more than she suspected. "Would you please move?" she requested icily. "Unless you prefer to do without lunch?"

He continued to stare down at her, his expression changing only slightly before he reluctantly straightened, allowing her a narrow passage in front of him. "You mustn't mind me, Cathy. Charles should have told you I can't resist teasing young ladies. Forgive me?"

Kindness was the last thing she wanted from him just then. It stripped her of her defenses, and Sinclair MacDonald already made her far too vulnerable. "How entertaining for you, Mr. MacDonald," she said, avoiding the last part of his speech. He was still much too close. Holding her breath, she edged past him, her arm inadvertently brushing against his lean, taut body. She pulled back as if burnt, and practically ran the remaining distance to the cabin, dashing down the steps and collapsing on a cushion, her heart pounding. They would all be laughing at her up there, she told herself, wrapping her long arms around her knees and rocking back and forth. Nothing but silence came from the deck for several moments, and slowly Cathy's deep, shuddering breaths slowed to normal.

"Are you all right, Cathy?" Meg's voice was soft with concern and guilt as she followed her sister below. "I didn't mean to make matters worse. I thought—"

Cathy took a few deep breaths, whipping off her sunglasses in the darkness of the cabin. "You didn't think," she said bluntly. "You call *that*"— her tone was filled with deep loathing—"*that,* fairly good-looking? I suppose you'd describe Robert Redford as just all right."

"Well, I guess I understated it a bit. I just thought you should realize that a handsome man can be nice too," she replied defensively, dropping down on a cushion beside her sister.

"Sinclair MacDonald hasn't yet convinced me. Macho pig," she added bitterly.

"Well, I can't argue with macho, but I really wouldn't call him a pig."

"I would," Cathy shot back, rising from the cushion and wandering toward the porthole. Sin MacDonald was directly in sight, and for the first time Cathy allowed herself a long, leisurely look, trying to inure herself to his undeniable attractions.

He must have been at least six foot three or four, with broad shoulders, a trim waist and hips, and those long, beautiful legs encased in faded denim. He wore ancient topsiders and no socks, and the V neck of his polo shirt revealed a triangle of curling golden brown hair. Cathy had always detested hairy men; Greg had been smooth and hairless. But somehow the sight of those brown curls was having an inexplicable effect on Cathy—one she told herself was disgust. She found herself wondering how far down his stomach the curls went. She hoped he didn't have hairy shoulders.

And she hadn't even taken his face into account yet. The square chin, and the wide, sensual mouth beneath a broad mustache gave him a faintly piratical air. Add to that lean, weathered cheeks with that seductive single dimple when his mouth curved in a smile, a straight, decisive nose, laugh lines radiating out around those smoky, unfathomable, uncomfortably *kind* hazel eyes, and the combination was as potent a blend of masculinity as Cathy had ever been subjected to. The slightly long, curling brown hair had a splash of gray in it, and as Sin pulled his sunglasses from the top of his head and placed them on the bridge of his nose, Cathy bit her lip, turning back to her sister's knowing gaze.

"Macho pig," she repeated defiantly. "But a handsome one, for all that."

"I thought you'd see it that way," Meg said with a satisfied smirk. "Do you want to see what

Sin brought for us to work with? I brought a salad and French bread—he said he'd take care of the rest."

Cathy busied herself rummaging through the picnic basket on the pocket-sized table, pulling out a surprising assortment of things. "Does he have a cook?" she inquired silkily, unwilling yet to refer to Sin by name. Given the contents of the picnic basket, Sin's disclaimer of kitchen abilities seemed a blatant lie.

"Not that I know of," Meg replied. "He prefers complete independence and self-sufficiency, or so Charles tells me. Why?"

"There's a beautiful quiche here, a crock of pâté, an icy Soave, Russian black bread...."

"Sin would be sure to know the best delicatessens," Meg responded before Cathy's accusing look. "God, what a feast! It will be all I can do not to make a perfect pig of myself. Aren't you famished?"

Cathy forced herself to turn casually away. "Not really," she replied from force of habit, surprised to find she was lying. For the first time in three months she was actually looking forward to a meal. It must be the sea air.

"Oh, dear, you aren't seasick yet, are you? We're scarcely out of the harbor." Meg eyed her with concern.

"No, I'm fine."

"You should go out on deck and get some sun. I'm sure you won't be in their way."

"I'd rather stay here."

"You can't hide in the cabin all day, Cathy!" Meg cried in exasperation.

"I can do anything I damn please," she shot back. "I feel trapped, maneuvered, *set up,* and I don't like it."

"So you're going to sulk and ruin the entire day?"

There was a long silence. Cathy turned to her angry sister, suddenly contrite. "I'm sorry I'm such a wet blanket, Meggie," she murmured. "I'll make an effort, I promise. Just give me a few minutes, okay? We don't want to eat for a while yet, anyway, do we?"

Meg's piquant face softened. "No, sweetie. We can wait as long as you want. I'll go topside and give you a few minutes to pull yourself together. Unless you'd rather talk?" She offered it tentatively, knowing from experience not to push her sister toward confidences before she was ready.

"Not now, Meg. And definitely not here. Tell Charles and Macho-Man I'll be out shortly, okay?" Wearily she pushed her silky blond hair away from her pale face.

A moment later she was blessedly alone in the tiny cabin. It was very quiet—the creak of the wood, the *snap-snap* of the sails overhead, the small, subtle sounds of wind and water against the sleek lines of the boat. And the sound of voices, soft, easy camaraderie with shared laughter floating down to her. *I should be out there,* she thought disconsolately, *not sitting alone in this tiny cabin the way I've been sitting alone in my apartment for the last three months. Surely Greg wasn't worth such prolonged mourning?*

Reluctantly she looked down at her clothing. Pale beige linen pants, a thin cotton knit shirt in a subdued gray, and running shoes made up her outfit. It would be too cold out there, she decided, wandering around the small room, peering with never ceasing fascination at the complete compactness of the living quarters. From the pocket-sized galley, miniature bathroom or head, and comfortable, blue-duck covered bunks, it was efficient and welcoming. Stepping past the head, she peered through the door into the forward cabin, then hastily backed away. The master cabin consisted of a large mattress, covered by a duvet, and nothing else. The perfect spot for a sybaritic weekend, she thought with an odd combination of nervousness and contempt, and took another step backward, her slender back coming up against something tall, solid, and unyielding. She didn't have to turn around to know with a sinking feeling that Sinclair MacDonald had caught her peering into his bedroom.

Turning, she tensed, waiting for some crack. In the darkened cabin he seemed impossibly huge, towering above her, his sea-blown brown curls almost brushing the ceiling. His sunglasses were still perched on his nose, and Cathy wished she still had similar protection from his probing eyes.

She could only be grateful the dim, shadowed light hid her reddened complexion.

"Did you bring a windbreaker?" he questioned after a long moment, and Cathy's shoulders relaxed. "You'll be too cold without one—the breeze is pretty stiff."

"I forgot," she mumbled, dropping her gaze from his face. Unfortunately, in that tiny space, there was little else to look at besides his body, and she decided that concentrating on his stomach or anywhere else below would be unwise. She stared fixedly at the curling hair at the open collar of his shirt, keeping a blank expression on her face.

To her intense relief he backed away, rummaging underneath one of the bunks and coming up with an Irish knit sweater that would probably reach to her knees. He tossed it to her, showing no surprise as she adeptly caught it, and pulled another out for himself. "Put that on," he ordered casually, pulling his over his head. "It'll be too big, but it's the warmest thing I've got." Still she stood there, holding the sweater in motionless hands. He started toward the steps, turned and gave her a semi-exasperated glance. "Look," he said, running a harassed hand through his already rumpled hair. "I promise to stay at the other end of the boat if that's what's bothering you. Your sister and brother-in-law are really worried about you. It would be nice if you could make an effort to be sociable."

She hesitated for a moment longer. "I'll be out

in just a minute," she said finally, shrugging into the heavy sweater. "And you don't have to stay at the other end of the boat," she mumbled into the sweater.

He moved back, a glimmer in those hazel eyes. "What did you say?"

"I said you didn't have to stay at the other end of the boat," she repeated patiently, hoping he couldn't see the deepening color on her pale cheeks. "I'm sorry if I was rude to you." She placed her sunglasses back on her nose and gave him a trace of a smile.

His smile widened, the dimple appeared, and the laugh lines around his eyes crinkled behind the dark glasses. "That's perfectly all right," he murmured. "I'm quite rude on occasions too. Truce?" He held out one hand. Cathy stared down at it for a moment. Her father said you could always judge a man by his hands and his eyes. She had already observed that his eyes were kind and humorous, much to her dismay. The hand in front of her was large and capable and well-shaped, the fingers long and tapering, the nails short and well cared for, unadorned by any rings. She put her slender hand in his, feeling it swallowed up in his strong grip. He let go far too quickly, his hand reaching out to take her elbow.

"Shall we join the others and tell them the war's over?" he inquired, a trace of laughter in his deep voice.

"Might as well. I don't want to have to spend

the entire day in the cabin," she replied with a trace of her old spirit, and was rewarded with a laugh.

"Well, for that matter, I could always keep you company. I'm sure we'd have no trouble finding ways to spend the time," he said casually.

He must have felt her entire body stiffen through the light clasp on her elbow. Yanking her arm from his grasp, she started for the steps. "No, thank you for the kind offer," she snapped, shaking with an overwhelming rage and something not far removed from panic. She had barely taken two steps when his hands reached out and caught her, turning her to face him and holding her upper arms in an iron grip.

"Hey," he said softly, his forehead creased, "what's gotten into you? I was only kidding."

"Well, kid with someone else," she cried, knowing she sounded neurotic and completely out of control. "I don't need Meg finding someone to flirt with me to take my mind off my problems, and I don't need—"

He shook her, briefly but quite hard, and the words rattled to silence. "Let me make one thing clear," he said in his deep still voice that had a curiously enervating effect on her. "I flirt with almost every pretty lady I see, unless I'm with someone, and you, despite your monumental bad temper, are one of the prettiest women I've seen in a long time. I don't need Meg to encourage me, and she knows she wouldn't get anywhere if she tried. Is that understood?" When she refused to answer he shook her again, hard. "Is it?"

"Yes, sir," she muttered, with little grace.

He laughed then, loosening but not releasing his iron grip on her tender flesh. "Now are you ready to go above and be the nice, sweet girl I know you are beneath that bitchy exterior?"

He was smiling down at her, that beguiling little smile, and Cathy could smell the salt spray and the tangy scent of his cologne, combined with the intoxicating smell of his sun-heated flesh. She made a face. "Yes, sir," she said again, deceptively meek.

"Good," he said, leading her toward the steps. "But let me tell you one thing, my girl. You don't fool me for one moment."

"I wasn't trying to," she shot back, starting up the stairs. "And you, Sinclair MacDonald, don't fool me either." She didn't know why she said it, and she was totally unprepared for his response.

"Really? I wouldn't count on it." And he followed her out into the bright sunlight.

Chapter Three

After their disturbing little confrontation in the cabin, things were surprisingly better, Cathy realized as she leaned back against the duck-covered cushions out on deck. If she didn't know it was impossible, she would have said she was enjoying herself. The blueness of the sky, the sea all around them, the easy, non-demanding company, including Sin MacDonald, seemed calculated to relax her wary suspicions. Stifling a yawn, she shook her silver-blond hair about her shoulders, staring out at the horizon with a preoccupied air. The breeze was chilly, but Sin's sweater was more than up to the task of keeping her warm. She would have liked to dispense with it—it was a toss-up as to which would be more disturbing: chattering teeth and blue lips or the insidious scent of Sin's aftershave as it clung to his over-sized sweater.

"More wine?" Sin offered lazily, and for a moment Cathy hesitated. The chilled white wine was delicious, but she had no head for alcohol. To be sure, Meg would take care of her and see that she got home safely, but . . .

"No, thank you," she replied politely enough, not missing the amused light in his eyes at her somewhat stilted courtesy. "I'm so full I couldn't move." As if on cue, Meg rose from her seat behind her sister and wandered forward to join Charles. Cathy tensed her muscles, prepared to join them, when Sin's broad hand reached out and stayed her. She sat back down on the shiny wood deck, unwilling to come in actual contact with him again. She was far too susceptible to his very potent charm.

"I think your sister and Charles would like some time alone," he said, making no effort to cross the three feet that separated them on the small square of deck. "They're still practically on their honeymoon."

"They've been married eighteen months," she shot back.

"As I said, they're practically newlyweds. You know, Cathy," Sin observed meditatively, "I am hardly likely to throw you down on the teak deck and rape you. Particularly with an audience."

Embarrassment and irritation warred for control, with embarrassment having a slight edge. She lowered her confused eyes to the deck, thankful once more for the sunglasses. "Is it teak?" she inquired with just a trace of agitation in her voice. "I assumed it was some sort of synthetic."

"I'm not much for synthetics," he stated, not bragging, merely as a statement of fact. And Cathy found she was inclined to agree. Everything about him was alarmingly real. "Why don't you relax?" he added. "I promise you you're safe from ravishment right now."

"I always assumed I was," she said boldly. "After all, I doubt I'm the type to interest a man like you."

"A man like me?" he echoed, arrested. "And what would you think that is?"

He had a lazy half-smile on his face as he leaned back against the bench, his long legs stretched out on the deck in front of him. Cathy hesitated, wishing irrationally that he would take off those shielding sunglasses, at the same time maintaining her own for protection from his all-seeing eyes.

"Afraid to tell me?" he taunted gently. "I know enough about you already to be certain you've made some very arbitrary judgments about me. I'd be interested in seeing how astute you really are. Not that I think I'd have a snowball's chance in hell of changing your mind once you make it up."

"You're quite right." She sat up straighter, curling her legs up underneath her to put even more distance between his overwhelming masculinity and her own frailty. "You strike me as someone who's very sure of himself."

He raised an eyebrow. "Overly so?" he inquired pleasantly.

"Bordering on it," she shot back. "You're used

to being found attractive by women, and can't quite comprehend that any poor female would be immune to your charms. You spend a lot of money on your pleasures, like your boat and the wine. You're probably quite vain, indolent, and you've already proven yourself to be sexist..."

He took this litany in quite good part, reaching into the cooler by his side and retrieving a beer. An imported German one, of course, Cathy noticed as further proof of his sybaritic tendencies. "I sound like quite a worthless fellow," he observed easily. "Haven't you anything good to say about me? No redeeming qualities?"

She considered this. "Since Charles and Meg like you, you can't be all bad."

"Dogs and children like me too," he offered meekly.

"You sail well," she continued sternly, ignoring his interruption. "And you have excellent taste in your expensive wines and such." She hesitated for a moment. For some reason Sin seemed to be waiting for more. Determined to be frank and bold and take the wind from his sails, she added, "And you're not bad on the eyes, either."

Whatever he had been expecting, that obviously wasn't it. A slow smile creased his tanned face. "High praise, indeed. You, however, are staying immune to my overwhelming physical attractions?"

"Completely!" she replied, edging slightly farther away from him. No matter how far she moved, he still seemed too close. She supposed he couldn't help being intimidating, he was so damned huge. "Just as you are to mine."

He pushed the sunglasses up to his forehead, surveying her through half-closed eyes, that smile still playing beneath his mustache. "What makes you think I'm immune to you, Cathy?" he asked softly, and the caressing sound of his voice sent a small shiver down her back, despite the heavy sweater.

"You assured me I was completely safe from—from ravishment, I believe was the word you used." She could feel the color come up in her face once more.

"That wasn't exactly what I said. I said you were safe, 'right now.'" He rose in one fluid, graceful movement, towering over her. "That doesn't mean I'll wait forever." And before she could reply with more than a gasp of outrage, he had made his way forward to join Charles and Meg.

Cathy stared after him for a long moment, awash with conflicting emotions. Emotions that couldn't be completely defined as outrage. There was something akin to excitement at the thought of Sin MacDonald directing all that tightly leashed masculine energy in her direction. Aghast at her own wayward thoughts, she hastily got to her feet, gathering up the debris of their luncheon and carrying it below. She couldn't tell whether it was the effect of the hot sun, or that intense look Sin Mac-

Donald was giving her from across the boat, but she suddenly felt it imperative to have a few moments to compose herself before subjecting herself again to that piercing, hazel stare. And her sister was far too knowledgeable, besides.

She delayed as long as she could, cleaning up the remains from their picnic, straightening the tiny galley and removing every last trace of their occupation. It was half an hour before she finally ran out of things to do, and she considered returning Sin's heavy sweater to the footlocker. But they were still about an hour out of port, and the wind had gotten substantially chillier as the afternoon shadows deepened. Obeying an impulse, Cathy slipped into the head, shut the door behind her, and turned to stare at her reflection in the mirror. The sunglasses covered fully half of her face, with only her pointed chin and hollowed cheeks and pale, tremulous mouth visible beneath the long curtain of silver-blond hair, now rumpled from the salt breeze. Taking off the glasses, she peered at her reflection. The green eyes were large and sad and wary in her pale, oval face, and the hours in the sun had brought forth a faint trace of freckles across her delicate nose. Ignoring the beauty that she had always failed to recognize, she decided she looked like someone recovering from a long illness.

With a sudden start she recognized the key word. Recovering. She never thought she would, or could, recover from the devastating blow Greg

Danville had dealt her heart and her pride, not to mention her body. But recovering she was, slowly, unsteadily, but quite definitely, thank you. The very thought was amazing. Crossing her eyes and sticking out her tongue at her Ophelia-like reflection, she planted the protective sunglasses back on her nose and joined the others on deck, curiously cheered by her short moment of insight.

"What are you looking so bouncy about?" Meg inquired casually, turning to survey her.

"Why shouldn't I be bouncy? It's a beautiful day, I've been entertained and well-fed. There's no reason I shouldn't be feeling good," she replied evenly, keeping her eyes averted from Sin's interested expression.

"No reason at all," her sister echoed, obviously mystified. "We've been hatching up a marvelous plan while you were below."

"Really?" She leaned against the railing, folding her arms across her chest and willing herself to relax.

"Several, as a matter of fact," Meg continued blithely. "First off, Sin's been planning on taking *Tamlyn* down to the Caribbean, and we thought it would be fun to accompany him. Charles would sail down with him, and I could follow by plane. We wondered if you wanted to come along. You know you've always loved the Caribbean, and I think you need to get away."

Several things flew through Cathy's mind, as her eyes caught Sin's seemingly occupied figure.

"Who's Tamlyn?" she blurted out, and then could have bitten her tongue at Sin's amused expression.

"*Tamlyn* is the most important female in my life," he replied, watching her expressive face beneath the glasses. "You've already berated me for spending too much money on her."

"I did?" she echoed, mystified. "Oh. *Tamlyn* is the boat," she realized belatedly.

"*Tamlyn* is the boat," he agreed with a smile. "Jealous?"

Her temper flared again, just as he had obviously planned. "God, you're conceited," she stormed.

"And you rise so nicely to the bait," he countered.

"Children, children!" Charles admonished, raising a restraining hand. "You two squabble like a couple of teenagers. Would you listen to your sister's idea, Cathy?"

"Okay," she agreed meekly, shooting a darting glance at the unrepentant Sin.

"I'd love your company, Cathy," Meg continued persuasively. "Sin and Charles will be spending all their time messing around with the boat, and you could keep me company. We could shop, and go exploring, and all sorts of fun things. Please say you'll come with me, Cath. I've hardly seen you at all since Charles and I got married and you met—I mean, I've missed you. We'd have so much fun, please, Cathy."

"Oh, I don't think . . ." she began vaguely.

"There's no reason why you shouldn't go. You're not working anymore, and there isn't anyone to keep you in town," Meg added with her usual lack of tact.

"But I'm not—"

"We won't be going for another month," Charles chimed in. "Not till sometime in November, when the rainy season is well past. I'd consider it a personal favor if you'd come, Cathy. I wouldn't feel right about abandoning Meg if you weren't there."

"Not that he should feel right about abandoning me at all," Meg laughed, sharing a tender glance with her obviously doting husband. "But you know what men are like. I doubt we'll even see them the whole time we're down there."

Cathy could feel Sin's speculative hazel eyes on her averted face. "I still don't think—"

"I think she's afraid we'll all have to crowd on the boat," Sin's slow, deep voice broke through. "Maybe you'd feel better about it when you realize we'll be staying at Pirate's Cove on St. Alphonse. This boat is definitely too small for four people, particularly when two of them scarcely know each other."

Meg added the most telling argument. "I mentioned the idea to Father and he thought it was terrific, Cath. Please say you'll come. I'll have a miserable time if I'm left to my own devices."

Cathy hesitated, torn by indecision. She knew

perfectly well that to agree would be succumbing to Meg's blatant matchmaking and tantamount to throwing herself at what now appeared to be a supremely disinterested Sinclair MacDonald. But for that matter, she too was supremely disinterested. So what could be the harm in it? If neither of them had any interest in the other, then there was no reason why they couldn't have a very pleasant time. And the warm trade winds and aqua water ought to do wonders toward her recovery, she thought, still savoring that word.

"She'll go," Sin announced suddenly, nearly catapulting her into disagreement once more. Shooting him a glance of irritation that had absolutely no effect, she nodded.

"I think I'd like that a lot," she agreed.

"Terrific!" Meg cried, enveloping her sister in an enthusiastic bear hug. "We're going to have a ball."

"This all depends on whether Father is feeling all right," Cathy warned, immediately having second thoughts.

"Pops is as strong as a horse, and you know it as well as I do," she shot back. "That tiny heart seizure has been the best thing in the world for him, forcing him to slow down. The pace he was keeping was killing him."

"I hope the boredom isn't finishing the job," Cathy replied. "Though I think he might actually be enjoying his curtailed activities."

"I have little doubt that he is. You know how he

loves having his grandchildren around," said
Meg, a faint blush rising to her cheeks. Cathy noticed the rise in color, and opened her mouth to
query her sister, then shut it again. Perhaps Meg
was still suffering from the memory of her miscar-
riage just six months after her marriage. This was
certainly not the moment for Cathy to bring it up.

"Well, that's settled," Charles announced,
his smooth, tanned face looking quite pleased.
"Why don't we all go out to dinner to celebrate?
You've been dying to go to that new Chinese
restaurant down by the water, darling, and
now's our chance."

"No, thank you," Cathy said hastily. "I really
have to be back. I—uh—promised Rosemary I'd
be there. She wanted some help on a sweater she
was knitting, and—and she was going to come
over."

Meg eyed her in surprise. "Since when have
you learned to knit?" she asked sharply.

"Since this summer. You promised me I'd be
back by late afternoon," she added, rather desperately, and then felt awash with guilt at the disappointment on both her sister's and Charles's
faces.

"Well, that's simple enough, then," Sin spoke
up. "I have to get back to town myself. I'll take
Cathy back, and the two of you can go out for
your dinner. I think an old married couple like
yourselves need a romantic dinner alone every
now and then, anyway." Cathy opened her mouth

to protest, then shut it before his quelling look. "You don't have any objections, do you, Cathy?"

She wished desperately she could think of one good reason not to accompany him. But there was none. None that she could bring herself to mention. Being in Sin's company with the protective presence of the Shannons was one thing; spending at least an hour in the confines of an automobile was most definitely another. The cynical expression on his lean, dark face told her he knew everything that was going through her mind, but there was nothing she could do. Reluctantly, she nodded. "That would be fine," she lied, and Sin's amused smile deepened.

Chapter Four

It was all she could do to control the little start of panic that swept over her as she watched Charles and Meg drive off into the gathering dusk. What in the world was she doing alone here on a deserted dock, trapped in the company of a man she had only just met, a man she found more than unsettling? What was it Meg had called him? "Somewhat dangerous," hadn't she said? And kind. Cathy stared after the retreating taillights, wondering if she could count on that vaunted kindness.

"The car's just over there," Sin's voice came from directly behind her, and she jumped, emitting a small shriek. Immediately his strong hands caught her arms, turning her to face him in the twilight shadows. "Hey, calm down. I didn't mean to startle you." The hazel eyes were staring down at her with a worried expression.

"That's all right." She pulled away from his grip quite easily. "I'm just a bit on edge."

The right side of his mouth curved up in a smile. "I'm sure you are. Would it help if I promise I won't do anything more than shake your hand? Scout's honor?"

"I doubt you were ever a scout," she scoffed.

"Your doubts are misplaced. I was an Eagle Scout, and the pride of my pack. So you see, you're perfectly safe with me." He gestured to the right with a flourish. "I'm afraid my car isn't quite as new as your sister's, but I promise it won't break down or run out of gas." He reached for her elbow to guide her to the car, but she nimbly sidestepped him. His grin widened.

"Suit yourself, princess. Follow me." He headed for the car, and Cathy stuck her tongue out at his tall, broad back before following him. He was already in the driver's seat of the small, green BMW. "I'd have held the door for you but I didn't want to expose myself to a blistering attack," he apologized with mock regret as she slid into the passenger seat and fastened the safety belt.

"There's nothing wrong with common human courtesy," she replied crossly. "It should simply go both ways. Women have just as much of a duty to be polite and considerate as men do."

"Exactly." His voice was dry as he started up the car.

It took Cathy ten full minutes to apologize. "Sin," she said, her voice small in the darkened car.

"Yes?" The voice wasn't terribly encouraging. He had spent the last ten minutes in silent contemplation of the highway, not even glancing once in Cathy's direction.

"I'm sorry if I've been rude. I've been going through a pretty hard time, but I shouldn't take it out on you." It took all her determination to come out with that, but she knew she had to apologize. No matter what her provocation, there was no excuse for her behavior.

"I know." At the understanding note in his voice Cathy's resolve nearly broke. And then his meaning came through.

"What do you mean, you know?" she demanded, horrified. "What has Meg been telling you? Damn it, I warned her—"

"Calm down. She only said you'd had a rough time of it recently. Your sister is worried about you," he explained patiently, as if to a child. "She talked to her husband and her husband mentioned it to his best friend. It's only to be expected."

"Only to be expected that when I make a fool of myself the whole world has to know?" she inquired bitterly.

"I hardly qualify as the whole world," he said reasonably. "And I know this will come as a great shock, but the previous love affairs of Miss Cathy Whiteheart are not of great importance to me. I have a great many other things on my mind."

"I'm sorry," she said again, and then laughed

ruefully. "I always seem to be apologizing to you. Maybe it would be better if I just kept my mouth shut to begin with."

"Better, perhaps, but not half as interesting." His hazel gaze raked her averted profile. "That was very noble of you, to let your sister and Charles go out tonight. I know a ride home with me was the last thing you wanted."

Guilt flooded Cathy's pale cheeks. "That's not true."

"Oh, then you wanted to be with me?" he inquired, a satanic lift to his brows.

"No, of course not. I mean—" She broke off, floundering. "I wish you wouldn't trap me into saying what I don't mean," she said irritably.

"Then maybe we'd be better off not talking at all," he suggested in a neutral tone.

"Better, but not as interesting," she shot his words back to him, and was rewarded with a laugh.

"Check and mate." He chuckled. They fell into a silence, but a surprisingly comfortable one. It was odd, Cathy thought, that neither of them seemed to feel the need to fill the silent car with idle chatter. Leaning back against the leather seat, she shut her eyes, the tension slowly draining out of her weary body. A moment later she was sound asleep.

She dreamed she was back with Greg, lying in his arms. It was a dream that had haunted too many of her nights during the past three months,

a nightmare that had no ending. Night after night
she had felt the warmth and love turn swiftly
into ugly, blinding hate and pain, physical pain as
she flinched from the raging fury that confronted
her.

But this time it was different. She felt the sweet-
ness of his breath on her face, the smell of his
skin, his aftershave strong in her nostrils, and she
knew if she opened her eyes that Greg's warm,
hazel ones would be smiling down at her. But
Greg had cold blue eyes, she thought suddenly,
struggling out of the mists of sleep, and he favored a sickly sweet cologne, not the spicy tang
that assailed her. Her eyes opened to stare into the
hazel gaze of her dream, but it belonged to Sin
MacDonald.

"Don't you think it's a little dark for sunglasses?" he inquired gently, reaching out and
taking them from her face before she had a
chance to gather her wits and stop him. The car
was parked outside her apartment building, and
he was hunkered down on the sidewalk, inside the
open passenger door, staring at her face in great
concentration. The streetlight was very bright
overhead, and she heard his sudden intake of
breath.

"My God, they're green," he murmured, his
voice low and husky. "If I'd known that I wouldn't
have let you wear those damned sunglasses for so
long."

"Give them back," she demanded, feeling

naked and horribly vulnerable in the face of his piercing regard.

"Cathy, it's almost nine o'clock at night. You don't need sunglasses at this hour," he said in an almost tender voice. "Besides, you're home."

She looked past him at the ancient building that held her apartment and three other luxury flats. "How did you know where I live?" she demanded suspiciously. "I don't remember telling you."

Sighing in exasperation, he rose to his full height, catching her arm and pulling her out of the car at the same time. "That's because I'm a Russian spy and it's my duty to know these things," he said wearily. "How come the paranoia?"

"Charles must have told you." Cathy satisfied her own curiosity, not noticing that Sin neither confirmed nor denied it. She held out her hand politely. "Thank you for driving me home," she said, her voice hatefully stiff and priggish. She knew she should invite him in for a drink, or even some dinner, but Sin MacDonald was a fairly overwhelming man, and at that moment she felt she had to be by herself, back in the safety of her apartment, able to hide from the confusing sensations and emotions that had assaulted her during the long, tiring day. And yet a perverse, totally irrational part of her wished he'd somehow prolong the evening. Force her to invite him upstairs, or drag her out to dinner. He hadn't taken no for an answer before.

This time, however, it appeared that he would.

He stared down at her politely outstretched hand, the sun-lines around his smoky hazel eyes crinkling in amusement. "That's right. I did promise to shake your hand." Clicking his heels together, he took her hand in his and bowed over it, for all the world like a Prussian officer. "Madame," he uttered in a thick, guttural accent, "the pleasure is all mine."

And without a backward glance he strode back to the driver's seat on his impossibly long legs, got in, and drove away. Cathy stared after him, an unaccustomed pricking in her eyes. What was she crying about? she demanded of herself angrily as she strode past the doorman, giving him an automatic friendly nod. Greg Danville had given her more than enough to weep about for the next few years; she didn't need to start crying about Sin MacDonald besides!

The apartment was still and silent as she let herself in, and unbearably stuffy after being shut up for the day. Out of habit she strode to the air conditioner, then made a detour to the long, Palladian windows that overlooked a mini-balcony. Pulling back the heavy curtains that had stayed shut the past three months, she opened the French door onto the cool night air. A fresh breeze ruffled her hair, and there was a scent of fall in the air. *Maybe the summer of my discontent is over,* she thought, wrapping her arms around her slender body.

At that moment she realized she was still clad in

Sin MacDonald's Irish knit sweater. Damn, she thought. Now she'd be forced to get in touch with him to return it. And for that matter, where were her sunglasses? Still in his hand, last time she'd seen them. Double damn. She'd have to call Meg tomorrow and find out how to reach the enigmatic Mr. Sinclair MacDonald. What a pain, to be forced to communicate with someone she found quite ... bothersome.

Humming beneath her breath, she moved into her kitchen and began assembling a gigantic sandwich. There was scarcely any food in the house—she'd have to remedy that tomorrow. Funny, but she hadn't felt much like eating since she couldn't remember when. And now, all of a sudden, she was eating like a weight watcher let out on probation. First stuffing herself that afternoon, and now she was wolfing down a sandwich that would have put a glutton like Charles to shame. Back to the refrigerator to discover, to her unalloyed joy, a single beer, the same imported brand that Sinclair MacDonald favored. *I'll have to get some more,* she thought, opening the bottle and pouring it into a heavy pub mug, and taking another bite of her sandwich. You never know who might turn up and want a beer.

The shrill ringing of the telephone interrupted her meal and she reached for the phone, spilling half of her drink in her haste to answer it. "Hello?" she said breathlessly around the remains of her sandwich.

"Cathy? Is that you? It's Meg." Her sister's voice sounded somewhat disgruntled.

"Hi, Meg. Who else would answer my phone?" she replied, taking a drink from her depleted beer.

"You're back so soon?" She sounded disappointed, Cathy thought. *But not as disappointed as I was when I answered the phone.*

"Of course I am. It's only forty miles from the marina," she said reasonably.

"But I thought Sin might take you out to dinner or something." Her tone of voice was plaintive. "You didn't scare him off, did you?"

"Of course I did," Cathy shot back. "Isn't that what I always do with importunate young men?"

"I wouldn't call Sin importunate. Or that young, either. He's older than Charles—probably around thirty-five or thirty-six. That would make him ten years older than you, so I hardly think that qualifies him—"

"Enough, Meg. You know I don't like matchmaking."

"Yes, ma'am. How did you manage to scare him off?" she questioned, a very real interest in her voice.

"It was quite simple. I don't think he was the slightest bit interested in the first place."

There was a long, disbelieving pause. "Well, we shall see. Sin isn't one to give up easily, and—"

"He's *not* interested in me, Meg. If I thought

he was, I wouldn't be coming with you to the Caribbean."

"But you don't dislike him, do you, sweetie?" Meg's voice was anxious.

"No, Meggie. I just have no intention of getting involved with someone at this point. If I ever do, I will let you know, and you can rush right out and round up all your eligible friends for my inspection."

"Well, all right. Maybe I should encourage Sin to bring a girl friend along, if you two really aren't going to hit it off. Though I don't know if I like the idea of some nubile young thing accompanying those two horny men on that very romantic boat for however long it'll take them to sail down. I've never seen Sin with anything less than a bona fide beauty."

"Do whatever you think is best. That might be a very good idea," she said, lying through her teeth. "Let me know what's happening, will you? Oh, and I forgot to give him back his sweater. Do you suppose I could drop it off with you and you could return it for me? And maybe get my sunglasses back?"

"Why don't you do it? I'll give you his number."

"No, please. I'd prefer it if you'd take care of it." All Cathy's earlier good humor was rapidly vanishing. "I don't want to see any more of Sinclair MacDonald than I absolutely have to."

"Hmm." Meg's voice was knowing. "I'll see what I can do. In the meantime, take it easy, okay?"

"Sure thing. Don't I always?"

"Not recently," her sister said wryly, hanging up.

The last tiny bit of sandwich went into the trash, the rest of the beer down the drain. Heading toward the bedroom, Cathy hesitated listlessly by the open windows, then shrugged and continued on her way. Tomorrow morning she could pull the curtains again.

She woke up suddenly, her slender body in the light cotton nightgown shivering in the predawn light. Another dream, another nightmare. With no Sin MacDonald to save her, she thought muzzily, huddling down under the light summer blanket. Still her body trembled, both from the cold and the aftermath of her nightmare.

Five minutes later, she sat up, sighing. A heavy flannel nightgown hung on the hook inside her walk-in closet, a cardigan sweater lay across the chair beside her, her quilted robe was just inside the bathroom door. Getting up, she padded all the way across the apartment in bare feet, out to the front hall. Sin's sweater lay there, where she had left it the night before. Pulling it over her head, she made her way across the apartment and got back into bed. The scent of her perfume mingled with the traces of his aftershave and the faint smell of the sea. Pulling the blankets around her, she shut her eyes, snuggling down into the Irish wool. A moment later she was asleep.

Chapter Five

Putting Sinclair MacDonald out of her mind was far easier said than done. During the next two weeks, Cathy found herself jumping every time the phone rang, racing to answer it, all prepared for the scathing denunciation that she had reworked several times during the ensuing days. But the phone had remained silent.

In the meantime she was torn. Part of her hated the thought of leaving the apartment and possibly missing a phone call, but the overwhelming emotion that haunted her was a need to escape. After three months of immuring herself in the four walls of her luxurious Georgetown flat, she found that she would go mad if she didn't get out for at least part of the day. She went shopping, buying unsuitable clothes that she would never wear, food that turned bad in the refrigerator and had to be thrown out. And for some obscure reason, she always kept a supply of imported German beer in the sparsely filled refrigerator.

By the second weekend after her daylong sail, the inactivity broke her will, and throwing her bathing suit and a change of clothes in the back of her small red Honda, she drove the forty miles to her father's estate in Virginia. Brandon Whiteheart's health had not been good, and Cathy never thought of him without a pang of worry.

As the youngest of Brandon Whiteheart's large brood, she had always held a special place in her father's affections, affections she returned fully. Her mother's death when Cathy was two years old had sealed her close dependence on her father, and Brandon had always found time to be there for her, despite his myriad interests. A brusque businessman, it had taken the gentle vulnerability of his youngest to pierce his hard-boiled exterior. Meg had still been young enough to benefit from his softening, but the three elder siblings—snobbish and overbearing Georgia, always so aware of her position as the daughter of one of the wealthiest industrialists in America; pompous Henry; and venal Travis, Cathy's least favorite of all her siblings—had been too well set in their ways. Too many years of parental disinterest had done their damage, and the three elder Whitehearts viewed their father's absorption with Cathy and her elder sister Meg with jealous exasperation.

All this was going through Cathy's mind as her little red car sped across the countryside. There was little doubt all three of them would be in residence.

Georgia and her husband Allen had moved in with Pops when Allen's business had gone bankrupt. Henry and his wife Milly were in the midst of moving, and were staying at Whiteoaks until their extravagant new house was completed. And Travis, dear, darling Travis with his little ways that bordered on sadism, came every weekend to ensure his inheritance. Despite the fact that Brandon Whiteheart had always been scrupulously even and fair in his dealings with his children, Travis could never find it in his heart to trust either his father's fairness or his siblings' greed. Since the heart spasm last winter Travis had raced down to Whiteoaks each and every weekend, eyeing his siblings with a jealous sneer and confining his conversation to snide remarks and sycophantic fawnings on his father. The absurdity of it was, Cathy thought as she pushed her silver-blond hair back from her face, that of all the wealthy Whiteheart children, Travis had done the best with his inheritance, more than tripling it in the last twelve years. Yes, she thought with a sigh, Travis would be there, and all the others, with the lamentable exceptions of Meg and Charles. They were too busy getting ready for their Caribbean trip. Maybe one afternoon with her father would be enough, she thought. Surely she could manage a few hours alone with him, long enough to assure herself that he was in good health, and then she could dash back to town before she got roped into one of those noisy, backbiting, unappetizing orgies known euphemistically as a family dinner.

As she turned into the long, winding driveway that led to Whiteoaks, a dark green BMW sped past her, too quickly for her to see the driver, but long enough for a shaft of unhappiness to mar her determinedly cheerful state of mind. Seeing a car so similar to his brought Sin back full force. Perhaps she could cancel her part of the Caribbean trip. Despite Meg's assurances that they would scarcely even *see* him, Cathy had her doubts. Circumstances would throw them into a "couple" situation, where the obviously disinterested Sin would be forced to act as her willing escort. The very thought made her blush with incipient embarrassment, and she told herself she would call Meg the moment she returned home. If she needed to get away, perhaps Hawaii would be a refreshing change. If only there weren't so damned many tourists marring the spectacular landscape! But doubtless St. Alphonse in the Caribbean would be equally tourist ridden. Maybe she would go to Europe.

"Well, Catherine, you were the last person I expected to see," her eldest sister's stentorian tones greeted her as she stepped lightly from the compact car and ran up the front steps. Georgia stood poised at the top of the wide, marble steps, her silvery blond hair perfectly coiffed as always, the blue eyeshadow heavy on her sunken lids, the thick coating of powder over the perfect White-heart features taking on a sickly mauve hue in the afternoon shadows. "And frankly, my dear, you don't look your best," she continued, tilting her head to one side in a deliberate attitude she had long ago perfected. "Do you think blue jeans and a khaki shirt are the proper garb in which to visit your father?"

Ignoring the rising temper always provoked by her contentious sister, Cathy clinked cheekbones dutifully, wondering if her pale, smooth cheeks had taken on some of Georgia's purple talc. "Pops is more than used to me," she replied evenly. "You're looking elegant as always, George," she added, not missing the tightening of her sister's thin lips at the hated nickname. "Is that a new suit?"

Georgia allowed herself a small preen. "Do you like it? Bendel's, of course. You really ought to do something about your clothes, darling. They're either disgraceful or terribly plain. No doubt you've brought some terribly staid off-the-rack thing for supper."

"I'm not staying for supper, Georgia," Cathy decided hastily, moving past her sister into the house. "And you know perfectly well that I don't care about clothes."

"You never have. You're not going to win a man that way, my dear. Take some advice from your sister, jeans and shirts will not do at all. I could also give you some advice on makeup. You don't take advantage of your looks, you know. You don't have to settle for being plain. With the proper makeup and clothes you could be passably pretty. I do wish you'd let me take you in hand."

"No, thank you, Georgia." Cathy accepted her sister's strictures with her usual stoic forbearance, having heard them all her life. If she had ever had any doubts about her possible attractiveness, Georgia had done her best to stamp them out, leaving Cathy feeling plain and gawky, not recognizing her own lithe charm and unusual beauty. Georgia had worked her black magic once more.

"Where is everybody?" Cathy queried, changing the subject quite firmly. "Is Pops resting?"

"You know your father, Catherine. Nothing can make him slow down. He's been conducting some very nefarious sort of business, and both Travis and Henry are livid. They've done everything they can to get him to confide in them, but your father does like to be mysterious."

A tolerant smile lit Cathy's face as she recognized her father's childish traits, a smile that turned her palely pretty face into a thing of beauty. "He's your father too, Georgia," she reminded her.

Georgia's beautifully shaped hands had curled into fists at her sister's smile. "Not so you'd notice," she said bluntly, turning her back on Cathy and leaving her without another word.

Cathy stared after her elegant, well-dressed back until her sister disappeared into the house, the all-too-familiar waves of guilt washing over her. "Damn it, Georgia," she whispered, "I won't let you do that to me anymore. It wasn't my fault."

"What wasn't your fault, darling?" Travis's slightly husky voice startled her into another polite curse. Reluctantly she turned to face him, wondering for not the first time how someone so endowed with physical charms and financial well-being could be so unpleasant. Her brother was just above medium height, with the same dark, wavy hair that Meg had, warm brown eyes, a beautiful nose and well-modeled lips. Unfortunately those lips were permanently carved in a sneer, and the brown eyes frequently glittered with malice.

"None of your business, Travis," she replied pleasantly enough.

"You should be used to your sister by now, Cathy," Travis purred. "She still hasn't recovered from the fact that Father couldn't care less whether she lived or died, and he thinks the sun rises and sets with you. Added to that the fact that you're far lovelier than she could ever hope to be, along with being seventeen years younger, and I think you can understand her irritable mood. She's usually much better when she's warned you're coming."

"I'm hardly lovelier than Georgia, Travis, and if you've been telling her so I wish you'd stop. Everyone knows that Georgia is the beauty of the family, and will be when she's eighty."

"All those people don't know my hermitlike youngest sister," Travis said smoothly. "What brings you down here?"

"I wanted to see how Pops was doing."

A frown creased his brow. "Don't you think we're capable of taking decent care of him, Cathy? Or are you expecting—"

"Travis, I just wanted to visit with him." Cathy interrupted him with a patience that was rapidly wearing thin. It was no wonder she avoided this place like the plague. "How is he?"

"Up to his ears in intrigue," Travis snapped, obviously nettled.

"By the way, who was that driving away as I arrived? In the green BMW?" she inquired casually, following him into the house toward her father's library, the only place he could still call his own in a house filled with visiting children.

"No one you know, little sister. Some business acquaintance of his, part of his hush-hush plan. Don't bother asking—even you won't get any further with him on this one."

"I have no intention of cross-examining him about his business. I doubt it would be all that exciting once I found out, anyway," she replied, stopping outside the paneled door to the library.

"Will we be seeing you at dinner, Cathy mine?"

A bitter smile lit her pale face. "Not likely. For some reason my family destroys my appetite."

"You don't look as if you've had much appetite recently, anyway," her brother observed sweetly.

"You know what they say, darling," she shot back. "A woman can't be too thin or too rich."

"And you know, from your experience with Greg Danville, that both of those things aren't true."

Cathy recoiled as if from a physical blow. "How do you know about Greg Danville?" she demanded hoarsely.

"You should know by now, dear Cathy, that nothing stays a secret in this family." Travis was unmoved by the reaction he had caused.

"Does Pops know about it?"

"Who do you think told me?" he purred. "Have you forgotten that Father employs a veritable army of private investigators?"

Slowly Cathy withdrew her hand from the antique brass doorknob, noticing with absent fascination that her slender, ringless hand was trembling slightly. "Good-bye, Travis," she said coolly, and turning on her heel, she strode out of the house without a backward glance. Travis's light, malicious voice floated to her.

"What shall I tell your dear Pops?"

She paused for only a moment at the front

door. "I'm certain you'll think of something," she replied without bothering to turn around. A moment later she was in her car, speeding down the driveway, away from the house, away from her hateful family. And away from her insensitive, prying, *controlling* father. Damn them all.

Chapter Six

The insistent ringing of her doorbell finally penetrated Cathy's heavy, drugged sleep. Without
bothering to check her digital clock glowing ma-
levolently in the darkened bedroom, she buried
her head under the feather pillow with a groan. Still
the buzz of the doorbell intruded. She pressed the
pillow closer over her head, swearing beneath her
breath.

Someone was leaning on the doorbell now, the
shrill noise penetrating the pillow, Cathy's hands,
and her aching head with a sadistic vengeance.
With a groan she threw the pillow across the room
and struggled out of bed, moving in a fogged stu-
por toward the front door.

It had been four in the morning before she had
slept. The thought of her father's betrayal had
been the cruelest blow of all, with her siblings'
customary malice a mere frosting on the cake.
From the moment she arrived back in her apartment, just after dark, the phone had begun to

ring, and ring, and ring, until she took it off the hook in desperation. For the first time in her life she wished she hadn't been so adamant in turning down the sleeping pills and tranquilizers her family practitioner had offered her. After all, everyone else took them, why shouldn't she? If she only had some, maybe she'd be able to sleep. Or at least stay awake calmly.

Even her most faithful friend, the television set, had failed her in her moment of need. The only thing on late night TV had been a turgid romance, far too well suited to her morose mood. The only alcohol in the house had been the imported German brew. It had taken two and a half beers to make her pleasantly tipsy, tipsy enough so that when she scrambled into her now customary sleeping apparel of shorty pajamas and Sin's Irish sweater, she fell asleep with only a few maudlin tears. To dream once more of Greg Danville, his blue eyes narrowed in rage as he stalked her, until she woke up with a muffled scream of terror in the predawn light.

It had taken another hour for her to sleep again. For two weeks Greg had been absent from her dreams, only to turn up now, when she least needed him. She had hugged her sweating body tightly, willing the panic to subside. She was safe, the door was locked, there was no way he could get to her.

The buzzer was still ringing in her head as she stumbled across the darkened living room, tripping over the pillows she had thrown, knocking over the stale, half-empty beer bottle in front of the television. Reaching the door with its damnable buzzer, she pounded furiously against the thick paneling.

"Shut up, damn you!" she shrieked. "I'll open the blasted door if you just give me a moment."

The buzzing stopped, leaving a silence even more deafening in her pounding head. Peering through the peephole, all she could see was a broad chest. She knew only one man that tall. She didn't even hesitate. With fumbling fingers she undid the three locks and flung open the door into the hallway. And there, leaning against the doorjamb, lounged Sin MacDonald, looking, if that was possible, even more overpoweringly handsome than he had two weeks ago. The faded denims encased his long, long legs, though this time he wore old cowboy boots in place of the sneakers. His lean, powerful torso was shown to advantage by a chambray western shirt, and the green sweater he had worn as a sop to the chilly weather brought out his hazel eyes. On his lean, tanned face was a tolerant half-smile, in one hand he twirled her missing sunglasses.

Cathy stood there, staring, her mouth agape, unaware of how completely appealing she looked, her silver-blond hair tousled around a sleep-smudged face, the long legs bare beneath the enveloping sweater. At the sight of her his smile broadened beneath the mustache, and he stood upright and strolled past her into the apartment, for all the world as if he belonged there, she thought wrathfully.

"I'm glad you're enjoying my sweater," he said mildly enough. "Isn't it pretty scratchy to sleep in, though? Or are you wearing something underneath it?"

Color flooded her face as she realized just how little she *was* wearing. She stood there, torn as to whether to order him from the house, or dash to the bedroom to put on something a bit more enveloping. Sin must have had the uncanny ability to read her mind, for he walked back past her dumbstruck body, closed the door, and turned to her, that lazy smile still playing about his mouth but not quite reaching the eyes.

"Don't you think you'd better put something else on?" he inquired gently. "Not that you don't look absolutely lovely, but the sight of all that delicious female flesh is a bit unsettling for a red-blooded American male."

"I—I—" She gave it up and fled to her bedroom, banging the door shut behind her.

She was in no hurry to put in an appearance after her embarrassing encounter. The clock by her bed read the unbelievable hour of 2:00 P.M., and she had obviously still been in bed. How did he know she was alone? She should have pretended there was someone waiting for her in the bedroom, someone who kept her in bed the better part of the day. Maybe that would wipe that amused smile off his face, she thought viciously, ripping off her clothes and turning on the shower, full blast. Maybe she could still pretend there was someone in here—after all, he was hardly likely to—

She had underestimated him. She had barely put her head under the heavy stream when his voice came horrendously close. "Do you like your coffee black?" he inquired casually.

Cathy let out a shriek of outrage as she saw his tall, strong figure through the rising steam of the shower. "Get out!"

"Do you like your coffee black?" he repeated, obviously unmoved by her outrage.

"Leave this room!"

"Not until you tell me how you like your coffee," he said easily, leaning against the sink, his eyes hooded in the hot steam. Cathy knew perfectly well the smoky glass of the shower made an adequate protection for those knowing hazel eyes, but at that point she wouldn't have put it past him to open the shower door to get her attention.

"I like it black and in private," she ground out.

He straightened to his full height, a good twelve inches over the top of the shower enclosure. She could see him towering over her, like Godzilla over a Japanese village, she thought furiously.

"Would you like me to wash your back?" he inquired sweetly. She took the wet washcloth and flung it over the door, watching it land with a satisfyingly wet smack full in his face.

There was an ominous silence, with nothing but the sound of the shower in the small bathroom. Sin dropped the washcloth back over the shower stall, wiped his streaming face on the thick blue towel she'd left out, and let himself out of the bathroom without another word. As Cathy quickly finished her shower, she tried to rid herself of the ridiculous feeling of guilt that Sin's silent exit had instilled in her. Perhaps she should have laughed it off, invited him to join her in the shower. After all, it wasn't as if she was still an innocent....

She dressed quickly in jeans and an oversized shirt before padding into the living room on bare feet. The room was transformed. Sin had pulled the drapes, picked up her spilled beer and the pillows and articles of clothing that she'd tossed about in a rage, and was now sitting on the sofa, his boot-clad feet up on the coffee table, casually drinking his coffee. Another cup was on the table in front of him, obviously meant for her. Cathy could see faint traces of water in his thick brown hair, but the hazel eyes that looked up at her were lacking anything other than polite interest.

"I decided you'd rather have your coffee out here than have me bring it to you," he said, his slow voice warming her. "I've already had one shower today."

With what grace she could muster she entered the room, picked up the coffee, and took a seat as far away from him as possible. "I have a temper," she allowed, taking a sip of the coffee.

"Apology accepted," he replied.

"There was none offered!" she snapped.

"No? That's what it sounded like," he said, unmoved by her wrath. "Why haven't you been answering your phone?"

"You tried to call me?" she questioned, her feelings warming somewhat. Maybe it hadn't been his fault that two weeks had gone by without a word.

"All last night and this morning," he confirmed, ruining her temporary mellowing.

"I didn't feel like talking to anyone," she replied coldly, taking another sip of coffee. It was extraordinarily good coffee; thick and black and strong, and she found herself leaning back in her chair.

"I gathered as much. I was hoping I could persuade you to have dinner with me tonight."

"I don't think—"

He overrode her objections. "We're leaving for St. Alphonse in a matter of days, with you and Meg following a week later. I thought it would be a good idea if I filled you in on the details. Where we'll be staying, what we'll be doing, what sort of stuff you'll need to bring."

"I've been to the Caribbean before," she said haughtily. "Besides, Meg could tell me all that."

"Meg and Charles have gone to visit his parents in Connecticut. Come on, Cathy, don't be difficult. There's no reason why we can't be friends."

Yes, there is, she thought silently, taking in the long, lean beauty of him. "Of course we can be friends," she said abruptly. "It's just..."

"You don't have anything planned, do you?" As she shook her head he rose to his full height. "Well, then, that's settled. I'll be back here around seven. Have you ever eaten at Champetre?"

Politeness forced her to rise and follow him to the door, politeness she wished she'd ignored as he towered over her, dwarfing her slender height. He was so close she could feel the heat emanating from his body, smell the faint, male smell of him, his bittersweet aftershave that had clung to the sweater. Keeping her face averted, she opened the door for him. One strong hand reached out and caught her willful chin, forcing her rebellious green eyes upward to meet his rueful hazel ones.

"Cheer up, Cathy," he said gently. "It won't be so bad. I promise you, I can be a perfect gentleman when the occasion calls for it."

"But will the occasion call for it?" she wondered aloud. And she also wondered if gentlemanly behavior was what she really wanted from him.

His smile deepened, so that the one, unforgettable dimple appeared beside his sensuous mouth. Suddenly, as if on impulse, he bent down and brushed his lips against her unwary mouth, his bushy mustache tickling her deliciously. It was so fleeting Cathy wondered if she dreamed it. Sin straightened and moved away. "I'm afraid, knowing you, that I'll have to be on my best behavior, or you won't come with us to St. Alphonse."

"True enough," she agreed, wondering if it really was. "Does it matter that much whether I come or not?"

He nodded. "Meg really needs you." They were not the words she would have chosen to hear. "See you at seven."

The door closed behind his broad shoulders with a tiny, well-oiled click. Cathy stood there, staring at the blank, white expanse of the door, lost in thought. *Haven't I learned my lesson,* she demanded of herself dazedly. *Haven't I had enough of handsome men to last me a lifetime?* With a sigh, she went back to her coffee, wondering what on earth she would wear that would both entice and discourage Sin MacDonald.

In the end she settled on a simple black silk dress, one that clung to her high, firm breasts, swirled around her gently rounded hips and hugged her slender waist. It was a very deceiving dress, seemingly demure until Cathy's graceful body moved beneath it. She both hoped and feared that Sin would notice.

She shouldn't have had any doubts. When he arrived at five past seven the look in his hazel eyes was both guarded and more than flattering. "That's a very dangerous dress, Cathy White-heart," he said in a low, deep voice after a long, silent stare.

She controlled the impulse to say, "What, this old thing?" She had bought the dress for Greg, bought it the day she returned back home from shopping to find him in bed with a strange woman. She had never worn it, and suddenly she was glad she had decided to ignore her misgivings. It wasn't the fault of the dress that she associated it with Greg. Besides, Georgia's cutting words had an unpleasant edge of truth to them. The remainder of the clothes that took up only a small portion of the space in her walk-in closet were unimaginative, unflattering pastels and flowered prints. She either looked like a schoolgirl or a housewife in most of them—even Greg at his most charming had been far from pleased with her wardrobe. But she had never had much interest in clothes. At least, not until recently.

"I'm afraid I don't have anything to offer you in the way of a drink." She made her voice cool and composed, something she was far from feeling. The mere sight of his tall, strong body, clad in gray flannel slacks, a black turtleneck, and a Harris tweed jacket that showed off the set of his broad shoulders was enough to send her pulse racing. His lazy smile and the promise in his smoky hazel eyes just about proved her undoing.

"That's all right, Cathy." He draped her jacket around her shoulders, the hands lingering for a delectable moment. "We can easily have a drink at the restaurant. I wouldn't want to put you out."

For one mad, impetuous moment Cathy knew the overwhelming desire to lean her head against that broad, deep chest and close her eyes, give over her troubles and responsibilities into his large, capable hands. She looked up, her green eyes meeting his for a long, pregnant moment, and then she blinked rapidly, moving away. "We'd better leave," she said, and her voice was noticeably shaky.

Damn him and the devastating effect he had on her. Tender amusement lit his eyes as he took her unwilling arm. "Certainly, Cathy. It's just as well. When I promised you could trust me to behave like a gentleman I didn't know you were going to wear that dress."

His skin seemed to burn through her clothing. She couldn't free herself from the nerve-shattering effect of his presence. In the luxurious confines of his BMW he seemed overwhelming, magnetic, and far more man than she was capable of dealing with at that point in her life. But the invisible wall she tried to erect toppled every time he smiled at her, touched her, and it took far too long to rebuild it each time. The day would come when she could no longer do so, and she didn't know whether she dreaded or longed for it.

She had steeled herself for an ordeal during dinner, fending off all that flirtatious charm, but as they took their seats in the elegant, secluded confines of the restaurant Sin suddenly became completely businesslike, treating her with a polite, distant charm that left her both relaxed and ever so faintly disgruntled. She scarcely tasted the delicious food he ordered for her, drank far too much of the excellent Bordeaux, and watched the candlelit shadows play across his strongly handsome face with bemused fascination.

That swift smile lit his face as he finished his brandy. "Have you been listening to a word I've said?" he asked. "You look like you're in another world, although it's obviously a much pleasanter place than the one you usually inhabit. What are you thinking about?"

"You," she answered forthrightly enough. "I know absolutely nothing about you. Do you work for a living?"

The smile deepened. "Now and then."

"At what?" she persisted.

"At whatever takes my interest at the time," he replied. "Any more questions?"

"If I had them, you'd be unlikely to answer," she shot back, nettled.

"How can you say such a thing?" he mocked gently. "Anyway, I bet I can answer them without your having to ask. I'm thirty-six years old, six feet four, two hundred and ten pounds, single, unemployed, unattached, and I drink Scotch.''

"Fascinating," she murmured.

"And then we come to you. You're five feet eight or nine, about a hundred and twenty pounds, twenty-six years old, independently wealthy, currently unemployed, unattached, and suffering from a mysterious and ill-advised broken heart. You drink imported beer and anything else I offer you, probably from a lack of interest rather than alcoholic tendencies. And for some reason I make you damned uncomfortable.''

"Maybe it's because you outweigh me by a hundred pounds," she retorted, draining her brandy glass in a defiant gesture. "And I'll have you know I'm the family wino. It's a deep, shameful secret, but I should have known I could never hide anything from you.''

"Hardly an alcoholic if it takes only two and a half beers to give you a hangover. You forget, I straightened up your living room today." He signaled for the waiter, tossing his linen napkin on the table. "And you're going to feel a lot worse after tonight. Two daiquiris, half a bottle of wine, and a brandy should make you practically comatose," he said affably. "I expect I'll have to carry you out to the car.''

"Don't count on it," she snapped. "I didn't have anything to eat last night. Anyway, I think

I'm getting used to drinking. What are you staring at?'' she demanded as his eyes narrowed with sudden intensity as they roamed over her face.

"How did your nose get broken?'' he asked abruptly.

Cathy's hand flew to her face. "I didn't think it was that noticeable,'' she said with a shaky laugh, determined to treat it lightly.

"It isn't. I've been staring at you for hours now and I just noticed. How did it happen?''

He wasn't going to leave it alone, she realized dismally. "Oh, I had it done. I thought it would give my face more character,'' she said breezily.

Sin continued to stare at her, his silence unnerving. "He did it, didn't he?'' he said finally. "Greg, I think his name was?''

There was a sudden roaring in her ears as the last vestige of color drained from her face. For a long moment she was afraid she would pass out. And then the need to run overcame her. Pushing back the chair, she grabbed her purse and ran from the room, past the crowded tables, blinded by tears, not knowing where she was going, only knowing that she had to escape from those all-seeing hazel eyes. When she reached the sidewalk in front of the restaurant she continued to run, panic-stricken, down the darkened street, the roaring sound in her ears so loud she didn't hear the sound of his pursuit until strong arms reached out and caught her from behind, spinning her around to fall against his broad, strong body.

Sin's arms came around her, strong and comforting, holding her trembling body against his with a solid tenderness. One hand came up and caressed her tumbled hair as she buried her face against his shoulder, wanting to hide away from the horrifying memories and this man's uncanny knowledge of her. But there was no hiding place, not even in Sin's arms, and after several long, shuddering minutes she pulled away, tilting her head back to stare up at him bravely.

The smile that curved his mouth and lit his eyes was curiously tender. He still retained a loose hold on her body, and one tanned hand reached up and caught her willful chin in a gentle grasp. "Sorry for trespassing," he said softly. "Do you want me to drop the subject?"

"Yes, please." Her voice came out in a husky whisper, and for a brief moment his hold on her tightened reassuringly. And then she was released.

"I'm afraid your precipitate exit rather precluded dessert," Sin remarked casually.

"I'm not really hungry."

"You may not be, but I'm still starved. And I'm sure you wouldn't say no to the best ice cream in the Washington area."

A faint glimmer of interest penetrated Cathy's abstraction. "Ice cream?" she echoed. "What kind?"

"Any kind that takes your fancy. Blueberry gem, maple walnut, apple-banana. Of course, the true test of a great ice-cream maker is my personal favorite—coffee." He took her elbow in the most casual of gestures and led her back toward the car.

"Don't be absurd," she replied, making an effort to match his light tone. "The real test of a great ice cream is vanilla. Anyone can make a decent coffee ice cream—all you have to do is add enough coffee. They're basically all alike anyway."

"Oh, you think so, do you? Wait until you try Benwards'. You'll never settle for bland vanilla again." He smiled down at her wickedly as he opened the car door for her. "You're too much of a woman to settle for anything as unexciting."

"As vanilla ice cream?" she retorted, knowing perfectly well he was talking about something far removed. As always she was much too aware of the tall, strong body next to her, even more now since she'd felt those strong arms around her, that formidably gorgeous body hard against hers.

"You're not a coward, Cathy I'm sure that once you decide what you want out of life you'll go for it with no holds barred," he replied mysteriously, shutting the door behind her and moving around to climb into the driver's seat.

"And I don't want vanilla ice cream?" she inquired.

His eyes met hers across the soft leather seat of the BMW. The streetlight above provided an eerie illumination, making Sin's face curiously brutal.

"It would be a waste," he said, and then turned his attention to the demands of city driving, leaving Cathy to stare out into the brightly lit nighttime streets of Washington.

Chapter Seven

It was almost three o'clock in the morning when they finally arrived back at Cathy's apartment. If the sight of the augustly demure facade of her building set off small alarms in her brain, then Sin's relaxed, friendly, completely nonthreatening behavior of the last few hours allayed those fears. It was almost as if, she thought with just a faintly disgruntled air, he had switched off his considerable sexuality like a light. The result had been more than enjoyable charm, but Cathy couldn't help but wonder when the panther would re-emerge.

The doorman nodded pleasantly as they walked back into the building, Sin's hand resting lightly on the small of her back. His touch was so gentle, in fact, that Cathy wondered why it seemed to burn through the thin material of her dress. "You certainly have a great deal of security around here," he observed as he followed her into the elevator. "I hadn't thought Georgetown was such a dangerous area."

"It's not. I just feel better knowing there's someone down there to keep out unwanted visitors. Speaking of which, how did you manage to get up to my apartment this afternoon?" she demanded.

"Speaking of unwanted visitors or security?" he returned, unabashed. "I have my ways, Catherine Whiteheart. You can rest assured, it wasn't your very ample security's fault. When I set my mind to something there's very little that can stop me."

A tiny, anxious shiver ran through her at his calmly implacable words, a strange sense of inevitability washing over her. "It certainly is late," she said nervously. "You should have told me the best ice cream in the area was in Maryland."

Standing in the close confines of the elevator he seemed even taller than his six feet four inches. The smile he gave her was no longer as innocent as it had been. "I didn't want to give you the chance to refuse."

"Yes, but did you have to force me to eat so much?" she groaned, holding her stomach in mock pain. "I agreed with you that the coffee ice cream was the best in the world."

"But how were we to know for certain unless we checked their other flavors?" he argued persuasively as the elevator doors opened with a soft swoosh.

"But twenty-four flavors?" she questioned plaintively, determined to keep up a light banter until she got safely behind her locked apartment door. "I doubt I'll eat for days." They were already at the shiny, black-painted door, and it was with a feeling of déjà vu that she held out her hand, remembering all too well her forced politeness in dismissing him the last time he saw her home. "Thanks for a lovely dinner," she said stiffly. "I'd invite you in for a nightcap, but it's far too late. There's nothing I want to do but fall into bed."

He cocked an eyebrow at her last sentence and she felt her pale face flush a fiery red. "Still keeping me in my place, Cathy?" he inquired gently, ignoring her outstretched hand. With an easy shrug he turned. "Good night." Seemingly without another thought he strode back toward the elevator, leaving Cathy staring after him with mixed emotions, foremost among them a perverse disappointment that he had given up so easily. As he waited for the elevator to return to the floor, he turned and leaned against the wall, hands in pockets, giving Cathy an absolutely devastating smile. And then he began to whistle.

The elevator arrived; the door swished open beside him. Those searching hazel eyes looked at the elevator, and then back at Cathy's motionless figure waiting by her door. Slowly he straightened up, and the panther look was back on him in full. He headed into the elevator, did a sudden about-

face and turned back toward her, stalking her like
the jungle beast he so resembled.

Before she had time to react he had pulled her
slender body against his, hard. Her hands were
caught between them as she instinctively raised
them to ward him off, trapped against his broad
chest. "To hell with keeping my place," he said
succinctly, and lowered his mouth to hers, gently
at first, as if not to frighten her. His arms were an
iron band around her slight frame, allowing her
room enough to move, but not to escape, as his
lips nibbled at hers, slowly, sweetly, drawing from
her a response she didn't want to give. One hand
slipped down her back to press her closer to him,
to make her fully aware of the strength of his response to her, and the slight loosening of his embrace allowed her enough leverage to free her
arms. She slid them up his chest, pushing against
him for a futile, angry five seconds, and then,
uttering a quiet moan somewhere in the back of
her throat, she slid them around him, entwining
her fingers in the long brown curls at the back of
his neck.

His lips left hers for a moment, trailing a line of
slow, deliberate kisses across her pale cheeks to
her ear. The tip of his tongue flicked out, tracing
the delicate outlines of her ear, his strong white
teeth capturing her lobe with gentle nips. "Open
your mouth, Cathy," he whispered as he moved
back to recapture her lips. Closing her eyes, she
obeyed, letting him regain possession of her

mouth even more intimately than he had before. His tongue explored every inch of her warm, moist mouth, demanding and drawing from her a response that she had never given another man. Her heart was pounding, her breath coming in quick, shallow pants, and her entire body trembled from pent-up desire. She could feel the flat surface of the wall behind her while every square inch of his body seemed burned into her flesh, and still he kissed her, as if he could never get enough of her willing mouth.

And then suddenly he moved away, out of her nerveless arms. Opening her passion-drugged eyes, she found his damnable hazel eyes staring down at her with a look of intense satisfaction.

He looked infuriatingly calm and collected, but Cathy couldn't help but notice his somewhat quickened breathing, and her yearning flesh had felt the imprint of his desire just moments before. He was scarcely as unmoved as he was striving to appear.

But his control was certainly a great deal better than hers. A disturbingly pleased smile lit his mouth beneath the mustache. "See you," he said lightly, and headed back to the still waiting elevator. Whistling, damn his soul!

She waited until the elevator had reached the bottom floor before she began to fumble through her purse for her key. Her hands were shaking so much she couldn't make it work for precious moments. When the lock finally turned she stumbled into her darkened apartment, racing across the living room to the French windows, pushing aside the curtains to stare out into the street.

Sin's tall body emerged from the entrance and strode casually, almost jauntily to his car, apparently as unmoved by the last few minutes as she was devastated.

As he opened the door to his car he hesitated for a moment, staring up at the darkened facade of the building. His eyes went unerringly to her windows, and in the bright streetlight she could see his strong white teeth flash in a grin. The same bright streetlight, she realized with belated mortification, that would doubtless illuminate her presence at the window, staring down at him like a lovestruck teenager. Quickly she let the curtain fall, moving away from the window as if she was burned.

The open door let in the only light in the darkened apartment. As she moved across to close and lock it, she reached a stray hand to brush her still trembling lips. Never in her life had she been kissed like that. Greg hadn't cared much for kisses, saving them for public occasions. Sin Mac-Donald had put more sexual energy, more sensuality and caring into that kiss than Greg had in the entire act of sex. If Sin's mouth was that devastating, what would the rest of him be like? . . .

"Stop it!" she cried out loud, trying to wipe such disturbingly erotic thoughts from her mind. But a short while later, as she lay sleepless in bed, the thoughts returned, the feel of his body against hers, the imprint of his questing mouth on her comparatively virginal lips. It was a long, long time before she slept. And when she finally did, her dreams took up where Sin had left off that evening.

Chapter Eight

The shrill, insistent ringing of the telephone broke through the mists of sleep. Cathy fought the nagging sound valiantly, and then was suddenly, completely awake. Her digital clock winked back at her—seven thirty. Immediately Cathy's thoughts flew to Sin, only to release them. Sin and Charles had left five days ago, were halfway to St. Alphonse by this time.

Struggling to sit up, she glared at the white princess phone by her bed.

"Hello!" Cathy snapped into the receiver, giving in to its demands at last.

"Cathy, thank God you decided to answer," Meg's voice came back over the line, blurred with worry. "I was afraid you might have unplugged the phone or something equally dismal."

"What's wrong?" Alarm shot through her body. "Has anything happened to the boat?" Horrifying visions of Sin MacDonald sinking beneath the angry Atlantic had her heart pounding and her palms sweating.

"The boat? Heavens, no. As far as I know, Sin and Charles are just fine. No, it's Pops. He's had another mild seizure."

Cathy didn't waste time with amenities. "Where is he?"

"At Littleton Hospital, but they're only going to keep him overnight. It's really not that bad, Cathy. They just want to watch him. Apparently whatever project he's been working on has been much too stressful. And I doubt Georgia or Travis has done anything to help matters. They tend to nag at him, and you know how Pops hates nagging."

"Have you seen him?" She hopped out of bed, the receiver tucked under her chin as she rummaged through her sparsely filled closets. "Can he have visitors? How does he look?"

"He looks fine." Meg chose to answer the last question. "A little tired, but not bad otherwise. He's resting right now, and the doctors think the fewer people here the better."

"But surely that doesn't go for me?"

"I'm afraid so." Meg's voice was uneasy with regret. "He really does need his rest, Cathy. I'm sure the doctors will let you in for a few minutes this evening. After all, you won't have another chance to see him for three weeks. Our plane leaves tomorrow evening and on this short notice I doubt we could change for a later flight.''

"Don't be ridiculous, Meggie! I have no intention of going to the Caribbean when Pops is sick," Cathy shot back. "I wouldn't be able to enjoy myself."

"You won't be able to enjoy yourself out at the house. Not with Travis breathing down your neck and Georgia set on an improving course. Pops will have a private duty nurse, and there won't be anything for you to do but sit in the middle of family squabbles. Besides, *I* need you, Cathy."

The thought of her resilient, self-sufficient sister needing her younger sibling was beyond comprehension. "Don't be silly—you're more than able to take care of yourself, and always have been. And besides, you've got Charles. Pops has no one that he can really trust."

"How do you think he'll feel, with a tug of war going on around him? You and Travis can never be in the same room for more than five minutes without being at each other's throats. And Georgia's getting impossible—she must be going through the change of life."

A reluctant laugh was drawn out of Cathy at the thought of her elegant sister allowing her body to betray her. "Don't be absurd—Georgia's only forty-three."

"But with her disposition she's old before her time," Meg shot back. "And she's more than capable of keeping the house in running order while Father takes it easy. You have to come with me."

"I can't."

"But what will Charles and Sin think?" Meg wailed. "They'll be expecting you to meet them there."

"Then their expectations will have to be dashed," Cathy replied coolly. "I can't leave when Pops needs me."

"Even though I might need you more?" Meg's voice was distraught.

"Meg, I can't! You, of all people, should know I have to be with Pops when he needs me."

But Brandon Whiteheart seemed to have little need of his youngest daughter after all. He greeted her from his hospital bed, looking deceptively robust despite the faint, grayish tinge around his mouth, with a gruff, "What's all this idiocy about not going to St. Alphonse with Meg?"

Unintimidated, Cathy shot back, "And what's all this nonsense about another heart seizure? I expected to see you flat on your back, looking at least slightly cowed, and instead you sit there looking hale and hearty. Faking again, Pops?" she queried as she bent to kiss his cheek.

"You know me, daughter, always looking for attention," he replied gruffly, pleased by her concern. "My doctor tells me I've been working too hard. Too much stress, he called it. As if anyone could live without stress in this crazy world today."

"I'm sure he's right. Travis has been telling me

you're up to your ears in intrigue—secret meetings, mysterious phone calls and the like. What's going on, Pops?"

"None of your business. Since when have I confided in a young thing like you about my personal affairs?"

"Don't try to look fierce with me, Pops," Cathy replied, unmoved. "Though I know from long experience that if you don't want to tell me anything I may as well not even bother asking. When are they going to let you out of here?"

"Tomorrow afternoon. And don't you bother about coming to see me—I know you'll be getting ready for your trip to the Caribbean."

"I would be if I had any intention of going," Cathy responded demurely. "As it is, I'll just move my things out to the house and await your return."

"No!" There was something curiously akin to panic in his husky voice. "I don't want you out there. I can't bear having everybody fussing over me."

Cathy's forest-green eyes met his calmly. "I can be just as stubborn as you, Pops. and if I've decided that I'm not going to St. Alphonse there's nothing you can do to make me go."

"You don't think so?" He met the challenge stonily. "We'll have to see about that. I'm not so sick that I can't still get exactly what I want. I have ways, daughter, that you wouldn't even begin to imagine."

"Really?" she shot back. "You should know by now that I'm more than a match for you."

"We'll see," he promised grimly. "We'll see."

The next day was far too busy to allow Cathy much time for second thoughts. There was no way in heaven she would spend the next few weeks at Whiteoaks unless armed with a large enough stack of novels to keep her safely occupied, away from the myriad delights of backbiting and gossip offered by her discontented siblings. Then she had to unpack her suitcases, dumping the warm-weather clothes and replacing them with jeans and sweaters to keep her warmer, although they were certain to turn Georgia pale with horror. At the last minute she packed Sin's Irish knit sweater. After all, he'd have no use for it down in the Caribbean, and he hadn't asked for it back.

For a moment she allowed herself to wonder whether he would regret that she hadn't come. Meg had maintained a stony silence since her final plea last evening, and Cathy couldn't decide whether she was relieved or disappointed. Heading down to St. Alphonse with Meg would have been playing with fire. Despite the fact that Sin MacDonald seemed scarcely interested in her, hadn't called her in the three days before he'd set sail, Cathy couldn't shake the remembrance of his devastating kiss in the hallway. If only she could decide what had provoked it. Was it a mere whim, a passing fancy, or a matter of habit? Maybe he was so unsure of his masculinity that he had to go about forcing it on any female who was less than interested.

Much as she wanted to believe that, it was too far-fetched. Sin knew only too well that beneath her cool exterior she had been fascinated despite herself. And she had yet to meet anyone *less* unsure of his masculinity.

She couldn't think of Meg without a wave of guilt washing over her. It wasn't often that her sister asked anything of her, and to have to turn her down was painful beyond belief. But Cathy's family ties were strong, and her thwarted need to be needed overwhelming. As long as she felt her father truly needed her, and Meg only *wanted* her companionship, then there was no question where her duty lay.

Glancing at the clock by her bed, she allowed herself a noisy, far from satisfactory sigh. Six fifteen, and Meg's plane would be leaving in less than two hours. Knowing her sister's almost excessive punctuality, Cathy had little doubt that Meg would already be en route to Dulles Airport, without having placed a last minute call to her sister, to cajole, to threaten, or at least to let her know she was forgiven. It was unlike Meg to hold a grudge, but in this matter she had used every trick she could to change Cathy's mind. Cathy had remained adamant, but now, as she watched her clock and sighed, she wondered whether she had made the right decision.

The ringing of her doorbell interrupted her reveries, the buzz shrill and angry in the silent apartment. It was amazing, Cathy thought as she closed her suitcase and headed toward the door, how expressive a mechanical device such as a doorbell could be. There was little doubt that whoever was ringing was quite furiously angry, a supposition that was borne out as a loud pounding began.

"All right, all right, I'm coming," she shouted crossly as she fiddled with the various locks and bolts. Before undoing the final one she peered through the peephole, encountering a broad, blue-clad chest.

"If you don't open this door, Cathy," Sin MacDonald's voice came unbelievably from the other side, "I swear to God I will break it down."

Hesitating no longer, Cathy slid the final bolt on the door and opened it. Standing there in all his towering six foot four glory stood a deeply tanned, furiously angry Sin. The last few days on the deck of the *Tamlyn* had turned his golden skin mahogany color; his hair was streaked by the sun, and his eyes, blazing as they were with anger, looked more green than hazel. He was still dressed in sailing clothes—faded denims, sneakers and a collarless white knit shirt opened at his darkly tanned throat. His teak arms were crossed on his broad chest, and the expression on his face was enraged.

If this man had been handsome before, the added days in the sun had made him well-nigh irresistible, Cathy thought dazedly, backing away from his panther stalk. "I—I thought you were halfway to the Caribbean by now," she stammered, cursing herself for showing how unnerved she was.

"I was, and still would have been if it weren't for your self-centered foolishness," he shot back. "When Charles called Meg last night she couldn't stop crying. Of all the selfish, adolescent gestures...." He ran an exasperated hand through his thick brown curls. "Don't you ever think of anyone but yourself? Meg needs you right now."

"Meg has Charles," she snapped. "And I fail to see what business it is of yours, or what you're even doing here, for that matter."

"I had to fly up for an important meeting, and I promised Charles I'd get you on that plane if I had to drag you kicking and screaming through Dulles Airport. If it were up to me I wouldn't give a damn what you did, but Meg and Charles need you." His voice was grim. "Now are you going to go pack your bags or will I have to do it for you?"

"If you take one step toward my bedroom I'll scream," Cathy replied furiously. "How dare you come in here and tell me what to do? Meg knows perfectly well why I'm staying behind, why I can't leave."

"And why is that? Because you're afraid to be around me?" he taunted with uncomfortable accuracy.

"Of all the conceited—!" Words failed her. Determined to calm herself, she took three deep, slow breaths. "I don't think we have anything more to say. I was in the midst of cooking dinner," she lied. "I'm going to continue, and when I come out I want you to be gone." Turning her tall, straight back on him with all the dignity she could muster, she strode into the kitchenette, praying, hoping, and dreading for the door to slam behind his retreating figure. Her nerves were strung taut as a wire, and when he came up behind her, his strong hands grabbing her arm and pulling her to face him with too much force, she grabbed the first thing she could to ward him off. Which happened to be a rather small, dull, and completely ineffective paring knife.

It happened so fast her mind blurred. One moment she had turned on him, brandishing the tiny knife, in the next he had spun her around and shoved her against the wall, her arm twisted behind her, the knife dropping from numb and nerveless fingers. For a moment she was dizzy from the pain, convinced her arm was about to be dislocated. And then she was released as Sin moved away, breathing rapidly in the tiny kitchen.

"That was a very stupid thing to do," he said shakily. Slowly she turned around to face him, her face paper white in the fluorescent light, her breath coming as rapidly as his.

"Yes," she agreed in a whisper. "It was." The look of the panther was back about him in full force, and for the first time Cathy was actually frightened of him. It wasn't so much the violence with which he subdued her pitiful attack. It was the speedy professionalism of it that filled her with horror and suspicions she couldn't even begin to name.

Sin's breathing slowed to a normal rate, and that dangerous look began to recede. He checked the thin gold watch on one tanned wrist, then met her wary gaze. "The plane leaves in an hour and a half. You have exactly fifteen minutes to get ready, or we'll leave without your luggage."

"I'm not going." She could have wished her voice was somewhat stronger than the reedy whisper, but she continued to glare at him defiantly.

Bending to pick up the knife and toss it back in the drawer, he took her arm in a gentle grip that belied the steel in his long fingers. "Haven't I made it perfectly clear?" he inquired silkily. "You're going to do what I say if I have to knock you unconscious and carry you aboard in a suitcase."

"You'd do just that, wouldn't you, if you thought you could get away with it?" she stormed. "You're nothing but a—a—" Various words flitted though her mind. What exactly was he? A terrorist, a gangster, a mercenary?

Apparently Sin was just as interested in her opinion. A faintly amused light entered his previously grim eyes. "I'm nothing but a what, Cathy?"

"A bully!" she said defiantly, her voice stronger.

The smile reached his mobile mouth beneath

the mustache. "I can't argue with that. Are you going to pack?"

She tried once more. "Give me one reason why I should accompany you?" she demanded. "Just one."

"I can give you several. First, because I'm a hell of a lot bigger than you are and I'm not giving you any choice. Second, because despite your martyred air, you know perfectly well that your father doesn't even want you around. So all this noble self-sacrifice is a joke. If you're worried about me being around let me assure you that I'll keep as far away from you as you like." Why did he have to look so desperately handsome when he made *that* magnificent concession? "But most of all, your sister really needs you. She's desperately afraid she'll lose this baby like she lost the other one, even though her doctor says it's fine for her to travel. She needs another woman with her, one she can trust and confide her fears in, and..." His voice trailed off before the combination of wrath and concern in her sea-green eyes.

"Someone she can confide in? It seems unlikely that I'm that person, since she didn't bother to confide the simple fact that she was pregnant again. How was I supposed to know why she needed me so desperately? Do you think I'm completely heartless? No, don't bother to answer that. Obviously you do."

Concern wiped the last trace of anger from Sin's tanned face. "I'm sure she meant to tell you before your father got sick. She only found out a couple of weeks ago, and she's been afraid to talk about it to anyone but Charles."

"And you," Cathy added bitterly.

"And me," he agreed. "Well, now that you know, what do you intend to do about it? Are you going to let her make the trip alone and worry herself sick?"

"Don't be absurd," she snapped. "I'll be ready in ten minutes."

"Make it five. I don't know about the traffic at this hour," he ordered lightly, taking her acquiescence quietly. If he'd gloated, Cathy thought, she would have gone for him again, no matter how efficiently he managed to repel attackers.

The ride to the airport was accomplished in silence. Sin kept his eyes straight ahead, all his concentration on rush hour traffic, while Cathy leaned back against the seat and closed her weary eyes, trying to remember what she had thrown in the one suitcase she'd had time to pack. For all she knew she'd end up in St. Alphonse with very outdated ski-wear, and she had the overbearing man next to her to thank for it. Stealing a glance at his uncompromising profile, she allowed herself a small sigh. No matter how she tried to hold on to it, the resentment had slipped away once she had committed herself to accompanying him. Perhaps he was right, that she had sought any excuse because she was afraid of him.

Well, she wouldn't have to be afraid of his attentions or that devastating light in his hazel eyes anymore. He had made it more than clear how little he thought of her. Self-centered, martyred, hadn't he called her? Well, perhaps he was right.

They had turned off into the airport complex when she finally found her voice and her courage. "Sin?" Her voice was slightly shaky. Sin kept his eyes straight ahead of him, his face expressionless. "I'm sorry." Her voice broke somewhat, and she cursed her vulnerability.

For a long moment it didn't appear that he heard her. And then, without taking his eyes off the road, his large strong hand reached out, covered hers, holding it in a gentle, reassuring grip that almost wiped away the last tiny bit of self-control she possessed.

For countless, breathless moments his hand held hers. In the darkness of the car her slender hand felt lost in his large, capable one, the calluses rough against her smooth skin, the strength and warmth flowing from his body to hers, calming and steadying her. It was like a tangible thing, the feeling flowing through them. And then, as they pulled up in front of the departure lounge, he gave her hand a brief, reassuring squeeze before releasing it to shift gears. And as Cathy turned her attention to the scurrying passengers, she couldn't shake the feeling that something incredibly intimate had just passed between the two of them. That knowledge was both enticing and threatening, and it was with a sense of relief that she watched as he stopped the car in front of a walk-way outside the air terminal.

"Meg's got your ticket." When he spoke his voice was entirely normal, and Cathy took her cue from him.

"She knows I'm coming?" she inquired steadily.

A flash of white against the dark tan signaled his amusement. "She knows I don't take no for an answer," he replied. "I'll see you in St. Alphonse."

"Aren't you flying with us?" She was startled into asking, then cursed herself for betraying her interest.

He shook his head. "I have some business to attend to, and then I'm flying back down to meet Charles outside of Miami so we can sail the rest of the way. We should follow you by two or three days at the most."

"Don't hurry on my account," she snapped. "We'll be just fine without you."

He threw back his head and laughed out loud, a warm, lovely sound on the autumn air. "I have little doubt that you will be. Try not to pull a knife on anyone before I get there. I might have difficulty extricating you from the results of such a foolish move."

"Don't worry. I'll save my knives for you," she replied in dulcet tones as she climbed out of the car. He seemed to hesitate for a moment, then, giving her an abrupt nod, he put the BMW back into gear and drove off, leaving her standing there, staring after him a bit woefully, her small suitcase clasped in her hand. Then, squaring her shoulders, she turned her back on his retreating taillights and went in search of her sister and her enforced flight to St. Alphonse. And as she moved through the crowds she was humming to herself.

Chapter Nine

There was a silvery sliver of a moon, hanging lop-sided in the clear night sky. As Cathy stepped off the plane onto the tarmac she stared up at the night, unable to shake a strange feeling of expectation. The air was velvety warm on her skin, a soft breeze blowing her hair away from her face, and she wanted to stretch out her arms and embrace the night and the sea breeze. Instead practicality reared its ugly head, and she turned back to her slightly green-tinged sister.

"That is the most horrifying landing I've ever had to sit through," Meg gasped as she reached the tarmac. "I thought for sure we were going to end up in the ocean."

"The landing strip was a little short," Cathy conceded, taking her sister's arm as she stumbled slightly. Cathy was feeling very protective now of her older sister; they had spent the whole flight talking about Meg's pregnancy and her fears. Cathy sent a silent thanks to Sin for having forced her hand; Meg *did* need her. "That's why we had to fly in on such a small airplane. But look on the bright side—at least we came in when it was dark. Can you imagine having to watch that landing in broad daylight?"

"Oh, please!" Meg moaned. "I may not leave St. Alphonse for nine months."

"Oh, taking off should be easier than landing," Cathy reassured her blithely. "And Charles will be with you to hold your hand." Unbidden the memory of Sin's hand capturing hers filled her mind and flooded her pale complexion. She averted her incriminating face. "Why don't you find a seat in the airport while I see to our luggage and a taxi? You look beat."

"I *am* tired," Meg admitted. "I don't seem to have much energy nowadays."

"That's perfectly normal for the first part of your pregnancy, isn't it?" Cathy couldn't keep the anxiety from her voice. "You've checked with the doctor and everything?"

"Perfectly normal," Meg reassured her with a smile. "Dr. Gibson says I'm strong as an ox and in perfect health."

"Well, stay that way, or you'll have me to answer to," Cathy threatened, her broad smile taking the sting out of her words. As she made her way to the baggage claim she reveled in her sense of well-being. It was a beautiful night, she would soon have a new niece or nephew, and she was away from Washington and the painful memories that she never could seem to shake. And whether Sin MacDonald disapproved of her or not, he was undoubtedly moved by her, and the thought of his incipient arrival caused a pleasant blend of apprehension and excitement somewhere in the vicinity of her stomach. And when she remembered the night he kissed her, the feelings made her feel dizzy.

It had been a tense few minutes after Sin left and Cathy searched the crowded airport terminal for her sister. She had finally caught up with her at the ticket counter. Meg had turned and met her searching gaze with a faint, guilty flush and a beseeching expression.

"You idiot," Cathy had announced succinctly, enveloping her petite elder sister in a tight hug. "Why in the world didn't you tell me?"

"I didn't want to force you to come," Meg mumbled, looking guilty.

"Oh, you didn't?" Cathy said lightly, skeptical. "Then why did you sic Sin MacDonald on me? He informed me he never takes no for an answer."

"I can believe that," Meg said soulfully. "Who in their right mind would want to tell him no? Anyway, I did try to tell you. Several times, in fact. But you were so caught up in Pops that you wouldn't listen." She gave her taller sister a tentative smile. "It's all right. I know how worried you were."

"I still should have given you a chance to explain," Cathy replied absently, her brain still distracted. "And I don't think you're right. Just because one wants to protect oneself doesn't mean one is out of one's mind."

"What?" Meg was justifiably mystified.

"You said no one in their right mind would say no to Sin MacDonald, and I said—"

"Oh, heavens, never mind that," Meg cut her off, the merest trace of mischief in her dark eyes. "You'll have more than enough chances to say no to him once we're in St. Alphonse. You can convince me of your sanity then. In the meantime, we're going to miss the plane if we don't hurry. Where's your luggage?"

"This is it." She had held up the small, carryon valise that contained heaven knew what.

"Is that all? I guess you'll have no choice but to live in your bathing suit."

"You won't like the one I brought. It's seen better days."

"Not that hideous flowering thing?" Meg cried. "The one that looks like a two-hundred-pound matron should wear it?"

"The same. You can always pretend you don't know me."

"Humph," Meg had replied unpromisingly. "I can see someone's got to take you in hand."

"Did I ever tell you," Cathy retorted in dulcet tones, "how much like Georgia you are?"

"Bitch," Meg said genially. "Very well, I'll

drop the subject. But not permanently, mind you.''

She went over that conversation in her mind as she unpacked her meager belongings. Moonlight was shining in the sliding glass door of her hotel room, silvering the sea-green carpet that was thick and soft beneath Cathy's bare feet. She was used to traveling first class, but she had to admit that Pirate's Cove Resort outclassed most of the other places she had stayed. The grounds had the absolute best landscaping, the kind that always looked natural and unplanned. The foyer of the hotel had a romantic, old-fashioned air to it. Any moment Cathy had expected to see Humphrey Bogart lounging near a potted palm, or Lauren Bacall slithering across the oriental carpet in clinging forties satin. And the rooms were absolute perfection.

Charles and Meg had a small, luxurious room on the second floor, with a king-size bed with brass headboard, silver-gray carpeting and a country French effect that was curiously suitable in that exotic climate. Their balcony looked out over the tiny cove from which the resort took its name, somewhat to the left of Cathy's view.

Her room was on the fourth floor, and nearly twice the size of her sister's. There were two king-size beds instead of one, with wicker headboards in place of brass and rough, natural Haitian cottons on the beds and at the sliding windows. The

Gauguin above the love seat was, to Cathy's amazement, authentic, and she vowed to take a closer look at the Degas in Meg's room.

"There you are." Her sister emerged from the bathroom looking pale. "I guess that plane ride was a bit more than I could take."

"I think the taxi ride did more of a number on your stomach than the plane," Cathy observed. "Listen, Meg, I've been thinking. It's absurd that I should be in this big lovely room by myself while you and Charles share the smaller one. Why don't we trade? I can't imagine why the hotel arranged it this way. Are you sure they gave us the right rooms?"

Meg's pale face flushed with something curiously akin to guilt. "I'm sure. Charles and I had that exact room last time we were here, on our honeymoon. I had to request it several months ago to be certain of getting it. Pirate's Cove is *very* popular."

"But are you sure you wouldn't rather have this room?" Cathy persisted. "It's absolutely gigantic for one person, and..." Her voice trailed off before her sister's miserable expression. "It is for one person, isn't it, Meg?" she asked quietly.

Meg shook her dark head. "Apparently not. The hotel got the reservation mixed up and they've put you and"—here she gulped—"Sin in the same room."

"Well, they'll simply have to make other arrangements. I'm not sharing a room with a man I

barely know, and I'm sure it's the last thing
Sin wants,'' Cathy announced with great assur-
ance.

Meg shook her head. "I tried," she said in a
voice that was little more than a whisper. "They've
been booked solid for months. There's not a
room or bed to spare, not here, and not on the
whole island. I'm sorry."

"Sorry?" echoed Cathy. "You've got to be kidding! I can't share this room with Sin! He's going
to think I planned it this way, I know he will. I
can't bear it, Meg. I—"

"Calm down," Meg's voice, eminently practi-
cal, broke through the rising hysteria. "Sin has
been treated to enough of your charm to know
that such a setup would be the last thing on your
mind. They won't be arriving for another couple
of days. If there's not a last minute cancellation
then you and I can share a room and Sin and
Charles can have this one."

"Don't be ridiculous. This is your first vacation
in ages—I'm certainly not about to break you up
like we were at summer camp. I'll fly back."

"You'll do no such thing, Cathy! You promised
me you'd keep me company, and I'm going to
hold you to it. If worse comes to worst Sin can
always sleep on the boat. He's done it before, and
I'm sure he wouldn't mind."

"How can you be sure there's not another room
on the island?" Cathy persisted. "I wouldn't
mind staying at another resort. As a matter of fact,

it might be easier. While Charles and Sin went off you could come over and—"

"You really are afraid of Sin, aren't you?" Meg mused. "He said you were, but I thought he was imagining things. Why don't you like him?"

"It's not that I don't like him," Cathy admitted, tossing herself down on the bed nearest the balcony and staring at the ceiling. "I'm just not ready to get involved with another man. The wounds still haven't healed from Greg."

An angry look closed down over Meg's usually cheerful face. "Some time," she said, "I would like to put out a contract on Greg Danville. The man should be shot."

"You know, Meg, I rarely even think of him anymore," Cathy admitted, surprised at her own truthfulness. "It's just the thought of anyone new that throws me into a panic."

"And what makes you think Sin is going to be that somebody new?"

Cathy rolled over to face her sister, pushing her silver-blond hair out of her shadowed face. "I don't know. It's probably just a combination of paranoia and wishful thinking," she admitted with a wry grin. "I'm too tired to sort it out tonight, anyway. I'm sure after a few days of having nothing to do but lie in the hot sun I'll be able to think of a way out of this mess. I could even stay on the boat while Sin enjoys this room and the nubile young ladies who will doubtless fall at his feet."

"What makes you think they'd fall at his feet?" Meg questioned curiously.

"Wouldn't you, if you were single?" Cathy shot back.

"You're single. I hadn't noticed you falling at his feet."

Cathy hesitated for a moment. "I hide it very well," she said quietly. "Now go to your room and get some sleep. I'm sure Junior doesn't appreciate these late hours you're keeping. It's no wonder your stomach is setting up a protest."

"But I want to continue this conversation," Meg insisted stubbornly. "Did you really just say—?"

"Forget what I said. Sometimes I talk too much. If I happened to notice that Sin MacDonald is an incredibly attractive man it's only because I'm not yet blind. That doesn't mean I'm going to jump into bed with him, it doesn't mean we have anything at all in common. It merely means—"

"Yes, I know," Meg interrupted, a twinkle in her dark eyes. "You can spare me all the rest of your denials and justifications. I'll just have to take you at your word."

"Do that." Cathy jumped from the bed, filled with a sudden restless energy. "Do you want me to walk you back to your room?"

"No, dear sister. You get a good night's sleep. We have an arduous day ahead of us, lying in the sun and broiling our delicate Whiteheart skin. I want you to be completely rested. Sweet dreams."

There was a distinctly mischievous look on Meg's face as she shut the door. Cathy strolled to the balcony and stared out into the moon-shadowed stillness. The quiet sound of the surf attempted to soothe her, but Cathy's nervous imagination was too strong for it. She knew only too well what she'd dream of that night. The nightmares of Greg seemed banished forever, to be replaced by the most lasciviously sensual dreams, all involving Sinclair MacDonald's six foot four body in erotic detail. Cathy wasn't yet sure which dream was more upsetting.

Chapter Ten

Lazily Cathy squinted into the mid-afternoon sunlight, the large sunglasses cutting the glare only slightly. Something nice and tall and icily fruity would be divine at that moment. As she burrowed deeper into the soft white sand she considered raising her hand in a languid gesture she'd observed others using. Within seconds a white-coated bartender would appear at her side, eager to cater to her every whim. There was something so wickedly sybaritic about Pirate's Cove, the way it encouraged indolence and self-indulgence. A self-indulgence that was frankly sensual. No, it would do her good to get up from her comfortable position and go in search of a drink herself. Besides, she'd been lying in the hot tropical sun for almost two hours. By using all her latent caution she'd managed to acquire a light golden color all over her body. Any more than two hours and that honey gold would turn to lobster red.

Sighing, she rolled over and struggled to her

feet, thrusting her arms into the terry cloth cover-up. Not that the old-lady bathing suit showed much, she realized with a flash of humor. Nevertheless, she just couldn't bring herself to stride around the sand or the hotel lobby wearing so very little. The terry cloth robe reached to her ankles, although it was slit up the side, halfway up her slender thigh. She ought to get a needle and thread and sew the slit, she thought absently, heading toward the shade and a cool drink.

There were a good half dozen single men sitting around the bar. All in bathing suits, exposing indecent amounts of flesh, most of it sunburned and flabby. For a brief moment Cathy allowed herself to wonder what Sin would look like in one of those brief excuses for a swimsuit, and then she shook that disturbing thought from her brain. The luxurious atmosphere of Pirate's Cove really had addled her brain.

Six pairs of eyes watched her approach. Even the enveloping white terry cloth couldn't disguise her long, shapely limbs or natural grace, and the large sunglasses beneath the silvery blond hair added to the mystery. Cathy recognized those avid expressions, and without missing a beat she did a right turn and headed back to her hotel room.

Meg had returned to her room an hour ago in search of a mystery novel. When she hadn't returned Cathy had presumed one of the all too frequent bouts of nausea had hit her. She would check on Meg, then head back to her room and order a piña colada from room service. A nice, cool shower before dinner would add just the right fillip to an already perfect day. And it was likely to be her last one. Sin and Charles were due tomorrow. The very thought of all the garbled excuses and explanations she'd be forced to offer before Sin's amused eyes brought a chill to her sun-heated flesh.

There was no answer at Meg's door. A momentary panic filled her, before she remembered her spare key. Opening the door a crack, she peered into the deserted room. Meg's bathing suit lay in a wet pile on the floor, her sundress from the morning tossed across the bed, a towel in the chair. Ever the neatly organized person, Cathy thought with amusement as she picked up her sister's clothing and hung it away. She must have gone back out, and somewhere they'd missed each other. Well, they would doubtless meet up again before long. In the meantime her skin was beginning to feel a little clammy in the wet bathing suit, and she hurried on ahead to her room two flights up, eager to get into clean, dry clothes.

Her feminine intuition must have been at an all-time low. She had locked the door behind her and come halfway into the room before the sight of Sin MacDonald brought her up short. And what a sight.

He was standing in the middle of the bedroom, clad only in a pair of faded denims that hugged his lean hips and encased his long, long legs. The entire expanse of bronzed torso was bare, and Cathy found herself mesmerized by the broad, mahogany shoulders, and the triangle of golden curls that started at his chest and then trailed down in a line beneath the belt of his jeans. Abruptly Cathy jerked her eyes upward, to meet those warm hazel ones that had haunted her dreams. And the moment she had dreaded was upon her in full force. She could feel her face turn red with embarrassment.

"Hi, there," he greeted her composedly. "I wondered where you were. Meg and Charles went off into town—something to keep her mind off her stomach, she said. I was just coming to find you."

"Uh—er—" Completely tongue-tied, Cathy continued to stare miserably as Sin pulled a polo shirt over his head, emerging with his brown curls tousled.

"Have you been enjoying yourself?" he inquired solicitously, sitting down on a bed, *her* bed, and putting on a battered white sneaker. "You look a bit sunburned. How is the water?"

"It's not sunburn, it's embarrassment," she said frankly. "And the water's beautiful. Look, we can't share this hotel room."

He said nothing, merely raising an eyebrow, as she stumbled onward. "It's not my fault, really," she stammered. "Somehow the hotel got the reservations mixed up, and they put us in together.

And they insist that there's not another room here, or on the whole island, for that matter."

"That wouldn't surprise me," he said calmly. "Even though it's not quite peak season, St. Alphonse is very popular."

"But you have to believe me, I didn't plan this. I don't like it any better than you do, and I know it's bound to put a cramp in your style, but there's nothing we can do about it. Meg offered to share her room with me while you and Charles—"

"Out of the question," Sin interrupted, a trace of a smile beneath his mustache. "I've had to put up with Charles's snoring for the past eight days. I more than deserve a break. That is, presuming you don't snore?"

"Of course I don't!" she said, affronted. "But I can't ask you to share this room with me. It wouldn't be fair to you. I'll take a plane home as soon as I can make arrangements."

"You'll do no such thing." He was off the bed in one fluid leap and standing in front of her, towering over her, that lean, panther look about him once more. She could feel the body heat emanating from him. "I know it's not your fault that the hotel got our reservations mixed up, and that's no reason to cancel your plans. Meg still needs you; you must know that after spending the last few days with her, Charles is devoted, but men leave something to be desired in a delicate situation like this."

"I don't know why you keep assuming I'd

know any more about this than a man would," Cathy broke in irritably. "After all, I've never been pregnant."

"I hadn't thought you had," he said mildly. "Maybe I'm romantic enough to think the mystical bond between all women comes through at a time like this. Meg needs you as much as ever, and I think *you* need this vacation. Despite this latest tantrum, you look a lot more relaxed than you did in Washington. Listen, we're both adults, and this room is gigantic, with two nice, large beds. I don't see why we can't manage to share this room very comfortably."

"But what if—if you meet someone?" she stammered, flushing beneath his ironic gaze. "And you wanted to take her to your room? Wouldn't that present somewhat of a problem?"

"I didn't come down here to 'meet someone,'" he mocked her delicate phrasing. "One-night stands have never been my thing. And if I happen to get carried away by my passions I could always go to *her* hotel room. The same goes for you."

"No!" she refuted the idea instantly. "I have no intention of ... of ..." Her voice trailed away.

"Well, then, that's settled. We'll live a very peaceful, celibate life while we're here. I'll be an eagle scout and you can be a nun, and we should get along beautifully. Anyway, I intend to spend most of my nights at the casino. I only allow myself to gamble two weeks of the year, and this is one of my weeks." He sat back down to put on the other aging Adidas.

Cathy let out a small sigh of relief, trying to squash the last traces of uneasiness. It should all work out after all. "I didn't know eagle scouts gambled," she said pertly.

He grinned at her. "That's the girl," he approved, somewhat mysteriously. "And I didn't know nuns wore gold earrings."

"By the way, roomie," she said after a long moment. "That's my bed you're sitting on. I got first dibs."

"Would you care to toss for it?" he shot back.

"My, my, you are going to spend all your time gambling, aren't you?" she mocked. "No, I don't want to toss for it. Possession is nine tenths of the law, and that bed is mine."

"Yes'm. I'm going down for a drink. Would you care to accompany me?" He rose to his full height, stretching luxuriously. Every muscle seemed to ripple beneath his bronze skin, and Cathy felt a sinking feeling in the pit of her stomach.

"No, thank you. I've been out in the sun too long as it is. I'm going to take a shower and then a nap." She managed a convincing yawn, despite the fact that her earlier lassitude had vanished.

"See you, then." A moment later he was gone, the door closed and locked behind his tall, well-shaped back. There was one problem with this situation, Cathy thought belatedly. It was all very well and good to share a room platonically, when Sin MacDonald had as much interest in her as if she were his sister. And an older sister at that.

But it would have been a hell of a lot better if she were equally indifferent to him.

Chapter Eleven

A long, cold shower might not have worked wonders, but by the time Cathy had washed the salt out of her hair and dried it in the soft trade winds off her balcony, then dressed for dinner and downed an icy piña colada, she was feeling up to facing almost anything. If only, she thought mournfully, she had managed to pack some of her new clothes. The one dinner dress was a boring cotton A-line with a high neck, an outfit that Georgia had once stigmatized as worthy of a grandmother from Hartford. It wasn't quite that bad, Cathy thought, twirling in front of the full-length mirror and posing coquettishly. The predominant colors were a shell pink that gave her skin a special glow and a sea green that matched her eyes. If the cut did nothing for her figure, well, then, at least it didn't make her look dumpy. Just sort of boring. It was fortunate she wasn't out to entice any man, wasn't it? she demanded of her reflection. Her reflection responded with a frankly skeptical look.

The bathroom had almost broken her resolve. Sitting on the shelf beside her meager stash of makeup was a brown leather shaving bag. Hanging on the back of the door was a velour robe, still damp from his shower, and on top of the sink was his toothbrush. It was all so uncomfortably intimate, just as if they were an old married couple.

But damn it, if he could survive this situation unmoved, then she would hardly be the one to cry coward. She could be just as cool and remote as he could, she told herself. She could take things in her stride....

It was a decided shock to watch all six feet four of Sin MacDonald stride into her bedroom as if he belonged there. As indeed, he did, Cathy reminded herself from her perch by the window.

"You're already dressed," he observed as he crossed the room. "Good. It won't take me long to change. I told Meg and Charles we'd meet them down in the Windjammer Room." He already had his shirt halfway over his head. Cathy allowed herself one furtive glance at all that sun-bronzed flesh before returning her attention to the sea outside the balcony. Tossing the shirt on his bed, he stood there, his eyes alight with amusement. "I bet I'm supposed to change in the bathroom."

"You guessed right. I may as well go down." Cathy headed toward the door, only to have her bare upper arm caught in his iron grip. He held her gently, but there was steel in his fingers, and

Cathy knew perfectly well she wouldn't escape until he was ready to let her go.

"You may as well wait for me," he corrected gently. "If you were rooming with another woman you'd wait, wouldn't you?"

Reluctantly she nodded. "I suppose I would."

"So, you see. You can be just as polite with me. Besides, I hate to enter a dining room alone. Makes me nervous," he announced cheerfully.

"Liar. Nothing short of a great white shark would make you nervous," Cathy joked back feebly.

Sin's grin broadened, and with his other hand he gave her a mock clip on the jaw. "That's it, kid. Don't let me browbeat you." He released her arm, grabbed a pile of clothes and disappeared into the bathroom, leaving Cathy to stare after him with a bemused smile on her face.

Dinner was a great deal more relaxed than Cathy had anticipated. For one thing, Sin seemed to go out of his way to be charming in an easy, comfortably nonthreatening manner. Not a glance, not an innuendo that wasn't entirely proper was cast in her direction. The subjects ranged from the lengthy trip down on *Tamlyn* and the various squalls the men had run into, to Meg's morning sickness to the myriad delights of the shopping on St. Alphonse.

"You mean to say you haven't been into town yet?" Sin demanded, astonished, as they were finishing their after-dinner coffee. "I don't believe it. I've never heard of a woman who passed by the chance to go shopping."

"Sexist," Cathy replied lazily. "Not every female jumps at the chance to spend a day wandering around crowded shops."

"Every one I've ever met has," he replied frankly. "You must be a very unnatural woman."

The lazy smile vanished from Cathy's face instantly as her blood seemed to freeze. *I won't make a scene,* she told herself. *I've already stormed out of a restaurant once, I won't allow myself to do it again. If I just take a few deep breaths it should be all right. One. Two. Three. There, I'm just fine.*

"Are you all right, Cathy?" Meg's worried voice broke through her abstraction. "You suddenly look quite pale."

Managing a light laugh, Cathy shook back her hair. "It's nothing. I'm just tired, I guess. Too much time in the hot sun. I don't think I'll come to the casino with you. Gambling doesn't hold that great an attraction for me anyway, and I'm quite exhausted."

"But it won't be any fun without you!" Meg pouted.

"Don't be silly. You'll have two handsome men at your side—you'll be in seventh heaven," she replied weakly. "And if you'll all excuse me, I think I'll go on up now." Before anyone could do more than protest she had slid from behind the table and headed for the door with as much speed as a graceful departure could manage.

The beach in front of the hotel was blessedly deserted. The moon was getting on toward full, shining down on the water and up the sand in a trail of moonfire. Slipping off her high-heeled sandals, Cathy moved down the beach by the water, the cool, wet sand beneath her bare feet soothing. It was very peaceful and quiet, with only the sound of the water lapping gently on the shore and the trade winds rustling the palm trees to keep her company. The lights of the hotel were hazy behind her, casting a soft glow over the beach. Heading for the farthest beach chair, she sat down on the wide chaise longue and pulled her knees up to her chest, wrapping her arms around them and hugging herself against the loneliness of the night.

His voice was gentle on the night breeze. "May I sit with you?"

She had felt his presence from a long way off, though his approach across the sand had been silent. Somehow she had known Sin MacDonald wasn't going to leave her to her misery alone on the beach. She kept her eyes on the shimmering water in front of her, wondering what would happen if she refused to answer. Would he take matters into his own hands and sit beside her? And then she could fence with him and perhaps take his comfort without having to put forth anything of her own.

But Sin knew her too well. He continued to stand there, calmly, patiently, awaiting her answer.

"Yes, please," Cathy whispered in a very small voice. Without a word he settled down beside her, his long, tuxedo-clad legs stretched out in front of him, the moonlight shining on his white shirt-front. It had been a considerable surprise to Cathy—how well he looked in evening clothes. She had imagined with his broad shoulders and craggy good looks that he'd appear out of place in anything besides corduroys or faded denims. But he had confounded that vague hope, appearing in black tie and looking, if possible, even more devastating.

The chaise longue, built for two occupants, was suddenly far less roomy. Cathy could feel the length of his thigh pressed against her hip, and the intimacy of it sent her heart racing.

Sin, however, appeared unmoved by her proximity. He leaned back and stared up into the starry night sky. "There. That wasn't so hard, was it?" he inquired gently. He reached out and took her hand in his large, capable one, and immediately Cathy felt the same feelings of power and warmth flowing through her. It was a comfortable feeling.

"No," she agreed. "Not so hard." They sat in companionable silence, and the sound of their breathing mingled with the sea and the wind.

After a long moment he spoke. Cathy could feel his breath stirring her hair, knew his probing eyes were upon her. "What did he do to you, Cathy?" The question was gentle, and for the first time in four months Cathy knew she could answer.

"You don't really want to know." She hesitated with a trace of grimness. "It's not very pleasant."

"I hadn't imagined it would be. I wouldn't have asked if I didn't want to know," he replied. His hand reached up behind her neck and she felt herself being drawn inexorably closer, to rest against his broad shoulder. One arm was around her, holding her close to the sweet-smelling warmth of him, as the other kneaded the base of her neck with slow, sure strokes. "I don't think you're going to get over it until you tell someone. And I think your roommate is as good a person as any. I'm not likely to condemn you or pass judgment."

Cathy could feel the tension drain out of her as she was enveloped in his calming strength. "I condemn myself," she said in a soft, bitter voice. "For being such a fool, and for going back for more. I should have known he was only interested in my money. There were enough signs of it. But I simply refused to see it.

"You see, I loved him. He was the only man I'd ever slept with, the only man I trusted enough to go to bed with. And he was so patient with my problems, and understanding, so how could I help but be grateful? He had to put up with so much from me, I felt I should . . . I should . . ." Her voice strangled to a stop, and she shut her eyes. Sin's gentle hand kept stroking the back of her neck.

"What problems, Cathy?" His voice was a

Harlequin reaches
into the hearts and minds
of women across America
to bring you

Harlequin American Romance.™

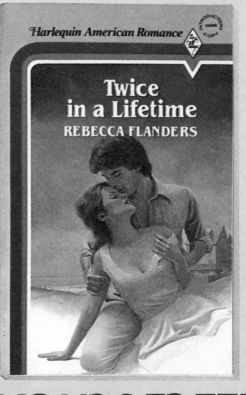

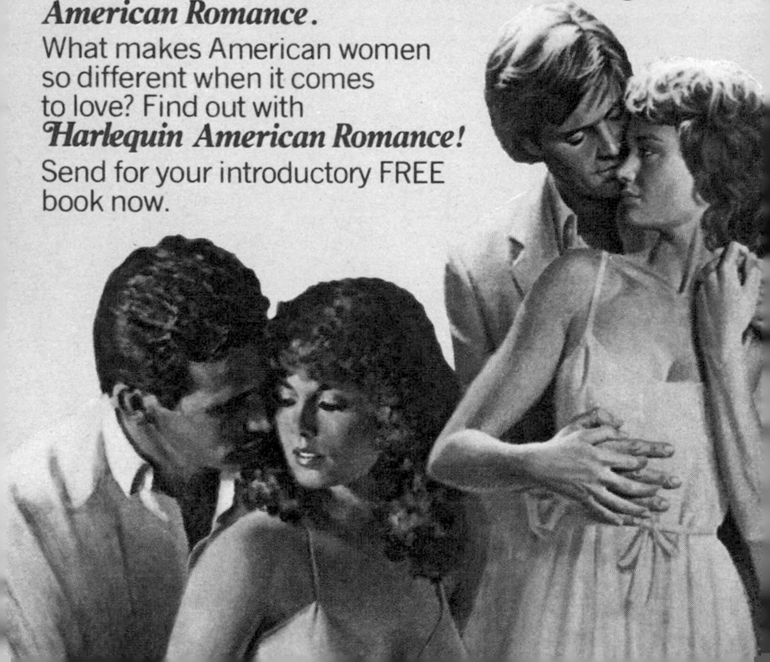

deep, gentle rumble beneath her head. "What did he have to put up with, that you should be so grateful?"

I don't believe I'm talking about this, Cathy thought mistily. *It's as if he has some magic power over me, enticing from me all my deepest secrets.* "I...don't enjoy having sex," she confessed finally.

"Says who?" His arm tightened around her, and Cathy could feel a strange tremor pass over his body, followed by another. Almost like a smothered laugh. But he couldn't be laughing.

"Greg. You see, I didn't—didn't respond at first. It was a long time before I could even enjoy the thought of making love with him. And even when I could, it took me so long to warm up, to respond to him...that he'd be finished. He said he didn't mind, but I know he did. And he told me I was unnatural, once when we were having a fight."

"No wonder you got upset at dinner. He sounds like a real charmer, your Greg. When did he break your nose?"

"I don't—don't remember," she said faintly.

"Why not?" He was inexorable. "It won't help you to block things out. The sooner you remember and face it, the sooner you'll get past it."

"It's not that—that I've forgotten the night," she confessed. "It's just that...it could have been one of several."

The soothing fingers stopped for a moment,

then continued in their circular, gentling motion. "He used to hurt you a lot?" There was a grimness in his voice.

"Only when he got so frustrated with me that he couldn't help himself. He was always miserable afterward." Cathy's voice was urgent with the need to find excuses. "Or at least, that's what he said," she added lamely.

"And how long did you put up with this?"

She bit her lip, stealing a hesitant glance up at his moonlit profile. She could read no condemnation in his shadowed features, only dark concern. She took a deep breath. The worst was over anyway—there was little more he could find out to disgust him. "Until the day I came home and found him in bed with a strange woman. In my apartment. In my bed. I never went back. I found another place to live and bought all new things and I haven't seen him since. So I suppose I'm not the abjectly miserable coward I thought I was. I did finally say no."

There was a long silence. And then his hand slid around from behind her neck and caught the side of her face in a gentle hold. "Cathy," he said softly, "did it ever occur to you that Greg did more than abuse you physically? That his lies about your sexuality were just that, lies to cover up his own inadequacy." His eyes were glittering down into hers in the moonlit night, and there was sadness and a great tenderness in them.

"But then why am I still so frightened of

men?" she cried. "And why do I freeze when anyone gets close? The very idea of making love makes me break out in a cold sweat, and ..." Her voice trailed off before the faint smile that lit his eyes and played on his face.

"It'll pass," he said softly, and bent his head down to hers, blocking out the moonlight. His mouth caught hers, gently, sweetly, his lips teasing hers with little nibbles, refusing to let her escape, until she opened her mouth beneath his to let him deepen the kiss, his tongue searching every corner of her mouth until she was overcome by a longing she had never felt before, except for a few moments in her hallway two short weeks ago. He was seducing her with his mouth, enticing her, and all this time his hands stayed decorously in place, one cupping her face and the other her shoulders, holding her slender body close to his. When she started to slide her arms up around his neck, to pull him closer, he suddenly broke off the kiss.

"That's enough of that," he said with a slight shake in his voice. "I think I've proved my point."

"You kissed me to prove a point?" Cathy asked in a dangerously low voice, her heart still pounding.

His smile broadened. "I kissed you because you're a delectably beautiful, incredibly desirable woman with a wonderfully kissable mouth, and because we're both sitting here in the moonlight with the Caribbean all around us. *And* to prove a point." He kissed the tip of her nose lightly. "Does that mollify you?"

"I suppose so," she said, not quite certain if she was telling the truth. "Shouldn't you be heading toward the casino? Are Charles and Meg waiting for you?"

"I've been dismissed, eh?" he inquired with a trace of mockery. "Very well, Catherine White-heart." He rose in one fluid motion, pulling her to her feet beside him. "I'll take off, after I make sure you're headed back to the room. I don't know that it's perfectly safe for you to wander alone on the beach."

"Especially with such a kissable mouth," she shot back.

"You've become a saucy wench all of a sudden," he laughed. "I told Charles and Meg to go on ahead. I'll follow them as soon as I put you in the elevator." Taking her arm in his loose grip, he led her back along the beach to the hotel entrance. "So tell me, Cathy." His voice was studiedly casual. "Have you heard from Greg Danville since you found him with your friend?"

A sudden, unformed suspicion caught Cathy off guard. "Why do you ask?"

"Just curious," he said easily. "Did he accept his dismissal without a fight?"

She hesitated for only a moment. "No, of course not. There was too much money at stake. He kept calling me, trying to explain. And when I refused to receive his phone calls or answer his letters, he sent me the most awful, vicious letter ... telling me just how useless and pathetic I was. I burned it, of course.''

"Did you memorize it?'' His arm slid around her waist protectively.

She looked up at him, managing a wry smile. "You know me surprisingly well for such a short time. I know parts of it by heart, quite against my will. Memory is a very stubborn thing on occasion.'' They were outside the elevator, the hallway deserted at that late hour.

"You need something new to replace those memories. New words, such as"—his lips brushed her forehead—"you have the eyes of a sea nymph, all blue and green mysterious depths. Or"—and his lips brushed her cheekbone—"your hair is like a curtain of silver rain. Or"—and his lips caught hers for a brief, lingering moment—"or ... but maybe I'll finish that later. Sweet dreams.''

Before she realized what had happened he had placed her in the elevator, smiling at her as the door slid shut, a disturbingly tender, maddeningly possessive grin. And then the elevator moved up, carrying her away from him.

Chapter Twelve

She slept very lightly that night, a part of her always alert for the sound of his footsteps, the opening of the door, the feel of his presence in the room. But time after time she'd sat up, wide awake, to find the bedroom still deserted. It was past four when she finally fell into a deep sleep, and when she first heard a quiet rustle of clothing her sleep-fogged mind insisted it was another false alarm. She turned over lazily, stretching her arms out into the darkness. And saw Sin towering above her dressed, no doubt in deference to her, in a brief pair of cotton running shorts. Her defenses momentarily abandoned, she smiled sleepily up at him.

"Are you still awake?" he demanded in mock severity. "It's five o'clock in the morning."

"Five?" she echoed hazily. "You must have had a good night."

He squatted down beside her bed, bringing his face level with hers. "I had an excellent night," he said lightly. "I won absurd amounts of money. The only way it would have been better was if you'd been there." He reached a tentative hand to brush a stray lock of hair out of her eyes, and she rubbed against him like a contented cat. He pulled his hand back as if burned. "Don't do that," he ordered sharply, not moving from his position by her bed.

Cathy burrowed deeper into the soft, comfortable bed, deciding not to question his irrational behavior. "Aren't you going to get in bed?" she questioned sleepily.

He seemed to hesitate for a moment. "Yes," he said, as Cathy felt the mattress sag beside her.

She sat bolt upright in outrage, but a moment later he had yanked her back against his body, fitting her against him, spoon-style, his long arms around her, holding her in place. "Go to sleep," he murmured in her hair.

"How dare you!" she fumed, fighting the delicious lassitude that washed over her. "You must be drunk. Get out of my bed!"

In answer he pulled her closer still into his warmth, and against her will she felt her body melt against his. He must have sensed her weakening, for he gave her a gentle, approving kiss on one bare shoulder. "That's right," he whispered, his breath hot on her skin. "All we're going to do is sleep together. For now." A moment later he was, to Cathy's mingled outrage, relief, and amazement, sound asleep.

She knew afterward that she was partly to blame for what happened. Still, he had insisted on getting in bed with her, against her vociferous protests. So was it her fault that hours later, half waking, half asleep, she had snuggled deeper against the long, warm body wrapped around her? That she had, sighing peacefully, turned in his arms and rested her sleepy head on his hair-roughened chest, had slid her arm around his lean waist and pressed her slender, unconsciously yearning body to his. One of his hands had moved down her back, to urge her slender hips against his, while the other gently cupped her chin. Opening her sleep-filled eyes, she gazed into Sin's probing hazel stare. He gave her more than enough time to turn her head, to elude his slowly descending mouth. Her arms tightened around his waist, her fingers splayed out across his leanly muscled back, as she willingly drew him closer. With a muffled groan his mouth met hers.

There was nothing tentative about this kiss, none of the reassuring gentleness of the night before. He kissed her long and deep and hard, with a kind of savage tenderness that was inexplicably arousing. Pressing her back into the soft mattress, he half covered her body with his, his long, bare legs holding the lower part of her body captive, as he plundered her willing mouth. His hand, which had been stroking her neck with long, sure strokes, moved down to caress one full, straining breast, his thumb rubbing gently until the tip hardened in fevered response beneath the silk gown. All her free will seemed drained away, leaving her a grateful captive of his knowing hands.

"Oh, God," he muttered against her soft mouth. "I want you so much." The hoarse words warmed her fluttering heart as she pressed closer.

Trailing fiery kisses down her jaw and the slender column of her neck, his mouth caught her breast, his tongue flicking over the rosy-tipped peak. Her nightgown had somehow gotten pushed down to her waist, leaving both breasts free for his sensuous attention, and as he moved his mouth to the other nipple she moaned deep in her throat. His hand trailed along one slender thigh, moving upward with inexorable determination, until he reached the innermost center of her being. She stiffened for a moment, then arched her back, reaching blindly for the waves of pleasure he was coaxing from her.

She slid her hands lower on his firm, muscled back, reaching the waistband of his shorts, and then stopped, confused. Greg hadn't liked her to be too bold—he wanted her lying there, passive, accepting his orders. She tried to blot out the memory, concentrating on Sin's wickedly clever hands and mouth, and a small moan of pleasure escaped from the back of her throat.

"That's it," he whispered against her silken skin. "Let me love you. I could make it so good for you, if you'll let me love you. Please, Cathy."

Through the sinking, swirling mass of sensations and emotions his enticing voice filtered through. "Let me love you," he'd said. Greg had another word for it. Many other words, all obscene, all necessary to him, the constant litany of filth as he hurt her....

"No!" she cried, yanking herself out of his arms and stumbling from the bed. "No, no, no, no!" she wept, shaking with panic and something else as she huddled on the floor, her arms wrapped around her shivering body. Pressing her face against the rough cotton bedspread, she sobbed in frustration and despair.

There was nothing but silence from the man in the bed for a long, breathless moment. Cathy was too miserable to look, certain he hated her, certain he was in a towering rage, so that when she felt gentle hands on her bare shoulder she flinched away in panic.

"I'm not going to hurt you, Cathy," Sin said gently, reaching down and lifting her shaking body into his arms, holding her against his broad, bare chest. Carefully skirting the bed, he moved to the upholstered loveseat on the far side of the room, sitting down very carefully so as not to disturb his comforting hold on her.

Cathy knew she had no right to accept his comfort when she had led him on so shamelessly. "I'm so sorry," she wept into his warm, bare shoulder, awash with guilt, fear, and frustration. "But I can't. I just can't."

"Shhh," he soothed, stroking her back with long, sure, calming strokes. "I know you can't. Not right now. It's my fault anyway. I didn't mean to rush you—I thought I had more control. It's just that you're so damned enticing." He reached a hand under her chin, forcing her tear-drenched face up to meet his. "Come on, Cathy. It's not so bad, is it? The big bad wolf stopped in time, didn't he?" He smiled down at her, a dazzling smile that melted the last of her panic.

"I guess so," she whispered, managing a shaky smile in return. He stared at her for a long, breathless moment, and Cathy wondered if he was going to kiss her again. If he did, if he took her back to that bed, she didn't think she'd be able to stop him.

Gently but determinedly he put her to one side, standing up and stretching, moving quite definitely out of her reach. "Why don't you get a shower while I go for my run?" he suggested, grabbing a sweat shirt out of the closet. "I'll see you at breakfast." He disappeared into the bathroom and emerged with a towel.

Cathy watched him from her perch on the love seat. "How much do you usually run?" she questioned, striving to put a casual note in things.

"Usually a couple of miles. This morning, however, I think I'm going to need to run twice that much, and take a nice, long swim. I'm afraid I have a lot of excess energy to work off." He bent over her, brushing a stray lock of hair out of her troubled eyes. "See you at breakfast?" His voice and touch were incredibly gentle.

"I . . . I guess so."

"Good. I'll be hungry," he announced with a grin that bordered just slightly on a leer, and left. Cathy watched him go with mixed emotions, foremost among them regret. And a stubbornly optimistic sense of promise.

To Cathy's immense relief Meg and Charles joined them for breakfast. To have had to make casual conversation facing Sin's tender, all too knowing eyes would have been a bit more than she was up to just then. Fortunately, the other three were all in excellent spirits, with more than enough to chatter about. Cathy would have thought her abstraction had gone unnoticed, had it not been for the small attentions Sin paid her. A soft touch on her arm as he offered her muffins, the reassuring momentary press of his knee against hers, the lingering of his fingers as he handed her the salt.

"I can't believe I feel so splendid!" Meg crowed. "It must be having you here, darling," she purred to her husband. "This is the first morning I've had without nausea in three weeks. I feel like doing something to celebrate. What should we do, Cath?"

All Cathy's attention at that moment had been directed to the strong backs of Sin's hands, the light splattering of dark hairs, the thin, long fingers, strong knuckles and well-shaped nails.

Hands that had already discovered ways to give her untold pleasures. Startled by Meg's question, she looked up, to meet Sin's knowing gaze. She blushed, a deep, fiery red. "I—I don't know. Whatever you'd like to do," she said lamely.

"I know what you can do," Sin broke in, the light in his eyes telling Cathy he had read her mind. "You can go shopping. There are a few things I want to do in town, and I would be more than happy to take you in. We can spend the morning on our various errands and get back here in time for lunch and an afternoon swim. How does that sound?"

"Perfectly divine," Meg breathed. "Don't you think so, Cathy?"

"Fine. But I don't really have anything I need to buy," she murmured.

"Now there I take issue with you." Sin's eyes were laughing. "What was that pink and green flowered monstrosity on the back of the bathroom door?"

Cathy's blush deepened. Sin's tone and words sounded so terribly connubial. "That's my bathing suit," she replied with a trace of defiance.

"I was afraid of that," he sighed. "Your only one, no doubt."

"One is sufficient," she replied haughtily.

Sin ignored her, turning to an amused Meg. "I can rely on you to see that she buys something more suitable, can't I, Meg? Suitably scant, I mean."

"You can, indeed," her traitorous sister agreed enthusiastically. "I've always told her it's a damn shame to have her lovely body and then cover it with old women's clothing."

"Am I to be consulted in this?" Cathy asked with dangerous calm.

"Oh, by all means," Sin said airily. "I'm sure Meg will let you have your choice, as long as you restrain your Quakerish tendencies. After all, this entire hotel thinks you're my woman, and I have *some* standards to maintain."

"You—you—" Words of outrage failed her. She had to content herself with a murderous glare that Sin met with a bland smile. A sudden, wicked plan began to form in her mind. She would buy a new bathing suit if he insisted. The largest, most old-fashioned, enveloping old lady's swimsuit she could find. Let him put *that* in his pipe and smoke it, she thought with satisfaction.

That plan, however, was much easier to envision than to carry out. The small, elegant boutiques that were scattered about St. Alphonse's main city of Verlage had nothing that would cater to senior citizens. The most enveloping of swimsuits were demure two-piece ensembles that still showed an alarming expanse of skin.

"Foiled again, eh, sis?" Meg questioned with amusement, having been the recipient of Cathy's evil plan. "Serves you right. Of course, you can always reverse your plan."

Cathy was in the midst of perusing an unbelievably scanty sea-green bikini, wondering who in the world would have the nerve to wear it. Although the scraps of material looked better suited to a precocious ten-year-old, the tag and label insisted it was her size. "How would I do that?" she inquired absently, holding the suit up to the light.

"You could buy the skimpiest, slinkiest swimsuit available. Something so outrageous Sin would be sorry he ever opened his mouth. The one you're holding looks like a good candidate," Meg observed.

"Oh, heavens, I couldn't do that," Cathy laughed, quickly shoving the suit back on the rack with a clatter of plastic hangers.

"And why not? You haven't got an ounce of extra flesh on your body. There's no reason why you, of all people, couldn't get away with something as skimpy as that."

Cathy's eyes strayed back to the rack. "He would be flabbergasted," she admitted with a wicked chuckle.

"He'd be speechless," Meg encouraged her. "And that's something I'd like to see. Sin always seems in complete control."

Not always, Cathy thought silently, retrieving the suit. "Maybe I'll try it on," she said aloud.

"Don't do that. If you try it on you might chicken out. You're a perfect size eight; you know that as well as I do. Just ask the lady to wrap it for you. The color matches your eyes perfectly."

On the verge of backing down, Cathy hesitated, torn. "It does?"

"Absolutely. Look, let me buy it for you, as a present," Meg urged.

"Nope. I'll buy it myself," she said with sudden decisiveness. "After all, it's time I learned to live dangerously. I..." Her voice trailed off as she headed toward the smiling saleslady. Her eye had caught the dress behind her. "Oh, my heavens."

"I see what you mean." Meg's voice was awed. "Who in the world would have the nerve to wear a dress like that? Not that it isn't beautiful. But gracious, it would cling to every single line and curve... and that hot pink! I've never seen such a seductive dress in my entire life." She reached out and touched a silky fold reverently, sighing loudly. "That's the sort of dress I've always wished I could wear. But I just wouldn't have the nerve." She eyed her sister's meditative expression with a secret smile, then added to the effect. "I couldn't get away with it, though. I haven't got the frontage to fill out that décolletage, and there doesn't seem to be any back to the thing at all. Why, it would fall right off me. But God, what a dress!"

"What size is it?" Cathy asked in a curiously resigned tone.

"Size eight, mademoiselle." The saleslady had rushed over, quite willing to be of service in the matter of the most expensive dress in the shop. "Would mademoiselle care to try it on?"

"Oh, why don't you?" Meg encouraged her eagerly. "Just for fun! No one will see you—it would be such a lark. How often does one come across a dress like that in one's life? It looks as if it was designed with your body in mind."

"No, I won't try it on," Cathy said with unshakable certainty, and Meg's and the saleslady's faces fell. She turned to her sister with a mischievous smile. "After all, as you just said, I'm a perfect size eight. If you would just wrap that with the bathing suit?" she asked the beaming shopkeeper.

By the time the two sisters met up with Sin and Charles they were absolutely laden down with packages, all containing clothes for Cathy. Silk blouses in jade green, hot pink, and deep plum, lean-fitting linen pants, evening sandals with tiny gold straps, and several pairs of quite the shortest shorts Cathy had ever seen filled their packages. Sin watched their approach with amusement, taking the bulk of their purchases in his arms.

"You didn't buy anything after all?" Meg questioned as they headed toward the Land Rover with its striped awning. "I thought you had urgent shopping to do."

"Good things come in small packages, nosy," he replied mysteriously, and refused to say anything more.

It took her a surprisingly long time to put all her clothes away after the light, sinfully delicious lunch served at Pirate's Cove. Silky little wisps of underwear replaced her serviceable cotton briefs and plain white bras; the pink dress she hid in the back of her closet. Her old bathing suit had mysteriously disappeared, thanks, no doubt, to Sin's meddling. One look at her body in the new, sea-green bikini was enough to send her rummaging through every corner of the spacious room. It was well and truly gone.

"I can't be seen in public in this," she gasped aloud to the mirror, tugging uselessly at the thin fabric. Her high, round breasts seemed about to spill from the thin, banded top, and the bottom was cut high on the thigh, slashed low across the hipbones, and just managed to cover her firm, rounded buttocks. If she didn't die of embarrassment she would undoubtedly strangle on it as it came off when she tried to swim. Of all the stupid, frivolous ideas. The color may have matched her eyes, but who was going to look at her eyes when everything else under the sun was exposed? She let out a helpless little groan, shaking her long blond hair down about her shoulders in a vain effort to provide more covering. The sun-tipped strands stopped several inches short of the rounded curve of her breast.

"I wondered what was keeping you," Sin's lazy voice came from the open door. "I was afraid you might have—" His voice trailed off as his wide eyes swept over the full, scantily clad length of her. Straightening from his lounging position in the doorway, he moved into the room, shutting the door behind him with an ominous little click. His face was completely unreadable in the early afternoon sunlight streaming in from the sliding glass door. Very slowly he walked all the way around her, his eyes raking her body in a fashion that in anyone else would have been incredibly offensive. With Sin, however, the effect made her tremble slightly with confused longing.

When he had finished his circuit and his eyes finally lifted to meet hers, there was an unmistakable light in their hazel depths, and the dimple in his right cheek was in full evidence.

"Are you trying to give me high blood pressure?" he asked mildly enough.

"I've seen people wearing less on the beach," she said in self-defense, not sure whether she actually had.

"At this particular moment I'm not interested in what other people are wearing," he said huskily, moving away from her and heading toward his dresser. "I guess my shopping was successful after all. I bought you a present." His eyes flickered briefly over her body, then back to her face again. "Something to go with your new image."

He tossed her a small, velvet jeweler's box. Startled, she caught it with one hand. "Don't look so frightened." He grinned suddenly. "It's not an engagement ring."

"I hadn't thought it was," she said with chilly dignity, wondering for not the first time how he managed to read her mind. Quickly she snapped open the lid. Nestled in the black velvet was a long, thin, gold chain, with a small, clear emerald. "What—what is it?"

He moved up close to her, his lean, strong body dwarfing hers, and took the box out of nerveless fingers. "It's a chain for your waist. It's supposed to be worn with a bikini." Suiting action to words, he unclasped the tiny clasp and drew it around her waist, his arms snaking around her. She drew in her breath at the potent touch of his hands on her bare flesh, and he laughed. "You don't need to hold your breath—it's more than big enough," he said casually, reclasping it and letting it fall. It rested just above her hipbones, the emerald winking up at her.

"Sin," she breathed, mesmerized. "I can't accept it."

"Why not?" He stepped back to admire the effect.

"Well, it's too . . . expensive."

"I can afford it."

"But it's too . . . intimate."

His grin broadened, threatening to split his tanned face. "Nothing's as intimate as that damned bathing suit," he said. "And I thought you'd learned I don't take no for an answer."

"You did this morning," she said breathlessly, then felt herself blushing.

He surveyed her for a moment, and then, before she could divine his intention, he moved toward her, put a hand behind her neck, and kissed her briefly and quite, quite thoroughly. Her mouth was seared by the contact, but before she had a chance to respond he moved away. "Now go on out and get some sun on that magnificent body of yours," he ordered lightly. "I'll be along shortly."

Cathy hesitated, still bemused by his kiss. He took a mock threatening step toward her. "Unless you'd rather spend the afternoon up here with me...?"

Grabbing her terry cloth coverup, far better suited to her new bikini than to her grandmother-suit, she ran.

Chapter Thirteen

It had been an exnilarating afternoon, Cathy decided as she surveyed her reflection in the bathroom mirror still clouded with steam from her shower. A perfect, golden glowing moment in time, when all that seemed to exist were the sea and the sun and the sand. And Sin's long, leanly muscled body lying by her side, the teak-bronzed flesh glistening in the hot sun. If she hadn't known better she would have thought he did it on purpose. That brief excuse for a swimsuit that stretched across his slim hips left little to Cathy's imagination, an imagination already overactive. The laughing light in his hazel eyes as he caught her hand and pulled her after him into the warm, salty water was far too knowing, but for some reason Cathy no longer minded. It was enough to be with him, laughing in the sunlight, her body drifting against his in the turquoise sea, collapsing exhausted side by side, arms brushing, legs touching, hands reaching, innocently, knowingly.

Sin had sat up abruptly, shaking the water out of his brown curls as he rested his arms on his drawn-up knees. He turned his head to meet her questioning, lazy glance as she lay there in the sand. Reaching out one tanned hand, he gently brushed the sand from her flat stomach, then smiled as she tautened her muscles in an involuntary reaction to his intimate touch. His eyes met her troubled green ones, and she had the uncanny feeling that he knew everything that was going through her head that afternoon. Knew it, and was amused by it. And yet the smile on his face was so tender as he leaned over her that she couldn't summon forth her usual outrage. Or even any fear, she thought with belated wonder. Sometime during the last twenty-four hours, some way, she had given her trust to him. And she knew with a sudden, blinding clarity that if he climbed into her bed that night she wouldn't stop him.

She took more than her usual care dressing that evening. Sin was sitting on the balcony, already in the elegant black dinner clothes that suited him so well, a German beer in one hand and a paperback thriller in the other. He'd barely looked up when she'd disappeared into the bathroom, content with lazily telling her to take her time. Such a domestic scene still unnerved her, filling her with all sorts of strange emotions, foremost among them a wistful longing for what was doubtless out of reach.

"Ridiculous," she told herself out loud, brushing a gold-tinted blusher across her high cheekbones. Sin MacDonald was hardly the marrying sort, and besides, she had only met him a couple of weeks ago. With an artfulness that she seldom employed she creamed her eyelids with a bronzegold, then darkened her lashes with a practiced hand. Pursing her warm red mouth, she eyed her reflection warily. With the gold-tinted makeup she looked vaguely exotic, and her silver-blond hair tumbled down her back in artful waves that owed more to the moist sea air than to a hairdresser's art. Taking a few steps back, she stared at the pink silk dress. It clung to every soft, ripe curve of her body, a body, she told herself firmly, that Sin had already seen far too much of in the bathing suit. At least this covered her, although the front hugged her round breasts beneath the décolleté and the back was nonexistent. It certainly had to be considered a bit more demure than the bikini, although looking at it Cathy was assailed with sudden doubts. Perhaps the cotton dress . . .

"Courage, ma vieille," she whispered stoutly. There was nothing wrong with her appearance. As a matter of fact, she looked almost beautiful that night. Her sea-green eyes glowed with anticipation, her mouth was tremulous with inner excitement. "You'll do," she whispered.

"Who are you talking to?" Sin's voice queried amiably through the door. "I thought you were alone in there."

Bracing herself, she opened the door. "I was

talking to my former self," she said bravely, strolling to her closet with a casualness that took her a huge effort to maintain. Her thin, gold-strapped sandals were there on the floor. They would have made her tower over Greg, but Sin would need more than a three-inch heel on his lady to feel dwarfed. *His lady,* she thought wistfully, sitting down on the bed nearest her and slipping on a sandal.

The thick silence penetrated her determined air of calm, and she looked up suddenly, still holding the second sandal. Sin was standing a few feet away, watching her with a completely unreadable expression on his face, his eyes hooded in the twilight evening.

"Is something wrong?" she inquired anxiously, and discovered that her heart was pounding. He took a slow, menacing step toward her, followed by another, and the look of the panther was about him again. He stopped when he reached the bed, and it took all Cathy's willpower not to cower back against the pillows. Determinedly she stiffened her spine, and looked way, way up into his enigmatic face.

"That dress," he said finally, "is outrageous." His voice was low and husky, setting her nerve ends to trembling.

"Outrageous?" she echoed, wondering if she should feel flattered or miffed.

"Outrageous," he confirmed. "You better hope your father never gets a look at it—he'd lock you away from all us voracious males. What do you call that color? Pink?''

She licked her suddenly dry lips. "I guess so." She still couldn't quite read his reaction.

"I've read there's a certain shade of pink that's supposed to be soothing to the savage breast. They've been experimenting with it in mental hospitals and jails, trying to calm dangerous inmates. I can tell you right now that isn't the shade of pink they're using," he growled. Suddenly he leaned over her, one long arm on either side of her, his face close enough to hers that she could feel his warm breath on her face, see the light in his eyes that removed the last trace of self-doubt.

"That color," he continued huskily, "makes me very, very dangerous. And you're sitting on my bed." Slowly, inexorably, his mouth descended, giving her more than enough time to escape from its overwhelming claim on her senses. But she had no intention of escaping. At the warm, wet taste of him her last defense crumbled, and she opened her mouth willingly to his probing tongue, her hands reaching up to clutch his shoulders in a convulsive grip. Slowly she felt herself lowered onto the bed as his body followed her down, his hands trailing up her silken body to catch her full, straining breasts. "No bra," he murmured against her mouth. "You shouldn't be allowed out." His mouth left a slow, deliberate trail of kisses down her neck as he rolled over and covered her slight body with his, one leg between hers as he continued his leisurely exploration of her soft, warm body. The peaks of her nipples had hardened beneath his practiced touch and with aching deliberation he let one strong hand trail down her midriff, across her abdomen and then below, his long fingers spread out over the pulsing warmth of her, his fingertips caressing lightly, teasingly through the clinging material, until she arched her back, pressing her hips against his hand in mute supplication.

Her hands slid from his shoulders to his chest, to meet the frustrating expanse of cloth that separated his body from hers. She wanted to feel his warm, heated flesh beneath her hands, let her fingers trail through the short curls of hair. She reached up to fumble with his tie when one hand reached up and caught her wrists, yanking them over her head and holding them there as he moved to cover her body completely with his. The clothes between them only seemed to heighten the sensations.

"Don't mess with the tie," he said lightly, his eyes smiling down into hers. "I spent almost half an hour getting the damned thing right, and I'm not about to let you undo all that hard work."

Cathy's breath was coming in short, heavy gasps as she looked up at him. Never had she felt more vulnerable, her body at his command, completely open to him as he continued to hold her arms above her head in a grip that for all its gentleness would allow no escape until he was good and ready. If it weren't for his slightly quickened breathing and the feel of his desire against her hips she would have thought this was no more than a game to him. But instinct, long dormant, told her this battle was just as important to him as it was to her.

"Sin," she began hesitantly, only to have her mouth stopped by the gentle pressure of his lips. Before she could move to deepen the kiss he had pulled away, getting to his feet with one lithe move and pulling her with him. She swayed for a moment, then caught herself.

"You'd better keep off the bed when you wear that dress," he said briefly, turning his back on her and running a cursory hand through his rumpled hair. "We're running late." He moved to stand by the door, ill-concealed impatience in his large frame.

Cathy started toward him, then realized belatedly that she still had only one sandal on. "You go ahead," she said. "I have to find my other shoe." It was nowhere in sight. Getting to her knees on the thick shag carpet, she peered under the bed, keeping her face averted. Confusion and hurt were warring with the remnants of warmth that lingered from his embrace.

"Where did you last have it?" He sounded subdued, preoccupied. Keeping her back to him, Cathy sat back on her knees, staring about her with unseeing eyes. "Don't worry about me," she said in a muffled voice. "If I can't find it I'll wear something else. Go on ahead," she repeated, her voice catching a tiny bit. She could only hope he didn't notice.

Two strong hands reached beneath her elbows and pulled her to her feet before turning her unwilling body to face his stern regard. "Cathy," he said wearily, "we're only playing this by your rules. There was nothing I wanted more than to stay in that bed with you just now. But you aren't ready, are you?" She refused to answer, staring mutely at her feet, and he gave her a little shake. "Are you?" he repeated, his fingers tightening on her soft, golden arms.

"No," she said, meeting his gaze fearlessly, wondering if she lied. The scent of him was a powerful aphrodisiac, that mixture of aftershave and sun-heated skin, brought out by the sensual exertion of the last few minutes.

His smile was just cynical enough to make her uncomfortable. "Your shoe is over by the balcony," he said coolly, releasing her arms and moving away.

She slipped it on as quickly as she could, not daring to stop by the mirror to check her appearance. She must look a wreck, she thought with a sigh as she preceded him into the hallway.

They rode down in the elevator in silence, Sin's expression abstracted. "Wait here for a moment," he ordered when they reached the lobby. He disappeared and Cathy wondered for a miserable moment if he'd abandoned her. It was probably no more than she deserved, after having led him on like that. A tease, that was what she was. Just a cheap, selfish little tease. She wouldn't blame Sin if he never wanted to see her again. He was probably trying one more time to find another vacancy on the tiny island of St. Alphonse rather than have to spend another night with—

Long, cool fingers pressed against her hot skin, lifting the silk curtain of her hair. "Hold still," Sin's voice murmured as she jumped nervously. The strong, intoxicating scent of gardenia assailed her nostrils, and she watched with mingled wonder and suspicion as Sin fastened the flower above her ear with deft fingers.

"A peace offering," he said lightly as he took her arm. "I don't usually sulk."

"Sin, I'm sorry..."

"Hush. You don't need to apologize," he murmured. "We can talk about it later."

"Good heavens, Cathy!" Charles greeted her approach with flattering amazement. "I always said you were beautiful, but that dress is a knockout."

"It certainly is," Meg endorsed her husband's approval. "It looks even better on than I would have expected. And that flower is just the perfect touch."

Cathy slid into the chair Sin was holding for her, her hair brushing his fingertips. "Meg helped me pick it out."

"Meg Whiteheart Shannon, I should have

known you'd be to blame," Sin mocked. "Always leading innocents astray."

"But you've got the flower wrong," Charles said with a sudden frown. "Didn't Sin tell you? You're supposed to wear it behind the right ear. If you wear it behind the left ear it means you're already taken. Engaged, married, in love, whatever."

Cathy turned to meet Sin's bland expression. He had always struck her as a man who left little to chance. "You should have told me," she said accusingly. She reached up to move it, but his hand forestalled her, the hard fingers cool on her heated flesh.

"Leave it."

Her eyes met his for a long, startled moment. And then she dropped her hand.

Chapter Fourteen

The music was soft and seductive, flowing gently around them. It was all Cathy could do to keep from swaying slightly in time with the hypnotizing rhythm. Determinedly she stared into her champagne glass, swirling the dregs, and keeping her attention as far from the dance floor as she could. Never did she think she would be jealous of Meg, but there she was, looking up into Sin's interested gaze, her still slender body cradled tenderly in his strong arms. Where she had absolutely no business being, Cathy thought, slopping a bit of champagne onto the tablecloth.

"Are you sure you don't want to dance?" Charles queried with a trace of anxiety.

"Not right now," she replied a trifle shortly, allowing herself a brief, painful glance in her sister's direction. Sin chose that moment to laugh uproariously at one of Meg's witticisms, and the unrestrained amusement was like a sharp pinprick to Cathy's already exacerbated temper.

"I can't imagine why Sin hasn't asked you to dance yet," Charles observed with tactless curiosity. "It's not like him to be remiss in these things."

"I think the problem, Charles," Cathy explained with deceptive calm, "is that you're assuming Sin and I are a couple. We happen to be sharing a room, but we might as well be strangers for all that. I assure you, our relationship is strictly platonic."

"Is that why Sin had your lipstick on his mouth?" her brother-in-law queried in dulcet tones. "I know you too well, Cath."

The music ended at that moment, before Cathy could come up with a suitable retort. And then Sin was towering over her, a bronzed hand on her arm.

She turned and gave him her frostiest glance. "Yes?"

He was unabashed. "Are you ready to dance?" he inquired evenly.

"I don't really think so," she drawled. Paying absolutely no attention to her demurral, the hand tightened, she was pulled unceremoniously to her feet, and moments later she was out on the dance floor, securely captured in his arms. One hand had captured hers, the other pressed against her waist, pushing her gently against his lean male strength.

"Now who's sulking?" He pulled her a tiny bit closer, with bare inches between their bodies.

"I am not sulking," she said defiantly. "I'm merely a little—a little . . ."

"Irritated?" he supplied sweetly.

She glared up at him. "That's as good a word as any," she shot back. "You've danced three times with Meg, and now, finally, you deign to ask me to dance, never for a moment considering that I may have lost interest—"

"I was waiting for a nice, slow one," he broke in, pulling her the rest of the way into his arms and pressing her head against his shoulder. She knew she should struggle, try to move away, but she did seem to fit so well.

"Why the sigh?" he inquired, his voice rumbling pleasantly beneath her ear.

"You're a bit too much for me," she confessed, lulled by the intoxicating warmth of his body and the slow, sensuous strains of the music. The hand at her back was caressing her lightly as it pressed her closer to his hips, and little tremors were dancing up and down her narrow and mostly exposed spine. The hand stopped for a moment, then moved onward.

"You forgot to take off the chain," he said lightly.

Cathy found she could be grateful to the dim light and her position against his shoulder. There was no way he could see the telltale color flooding her face. "I didn't want to," she whispered, and had the dubious satisfaction of having his arms tighten around her.

"Sin, darling!" A shrill, affected voice broke though her reverie, and she jerked herself away as if burned, to come face to face with a tiny, vivacious brunette. One red-tipped hand was on Sin's black dinner jacket, and the look on her sophisticated face was, to Cathy's mind, frankly acquisitive. "I couldn't believe it was really you! When I've been searching high and low for weeks now, all over Washington and New York. I never for a moment thought I'd find you here in St. Alphonse. Isn't this rather far afield for you, darling? I mean, it isn't your vacation, is it? You're always so terribly frugal with your vacations, when I don't see why you need to be. After all, what's the good of owning your own company if you can't do as you please?" Her light laugh rang out. By this time the music had stopped, the band had departed the bandstand for a short break, and Cathy longed more than anything to escape. But Sin's hand was still firm on her arm, not about to let her go.

"Hello, Joyce," he greeted her evenly when the flow of words had come to a temporary halt. "I hadn't expected to see you here."

"Well, of course you didn't, darling. And I scarcely expected to find you here either, though I remember the time we came down together...." She let the phrase trail meaningfully, more than aware of the effect her supposedly artless conversation was having on the female half of her audience. Her luminous brown eyes swept over Cathy's figure, a flash of envy for the dress clouding them momentarily. And then her red lips curved in a bright smile. "And who's your little friend, darling? I hadn't heard you were seeing someone new. Unless, of course, she's involved in—"

To Cathy's complete amazement Sin dropped his grip on her arm, taking Joyce's slightly overripe one instead. "Joyce VanDeiler, this is Cathy. I'll see you back at the table." With that hasty dismissal he turned and positively rushed the petite beauty toward the opposite end of the room. Cathy stared after them in mingled rage, hurt, and sheer surprise, before making her solitary way back to the table and Meg and Charles's interested faces.

"Who was the femme fatale?" Charles inquired. "I don't think I know her."

"Her name is Joyce VanDeiler," Cathy offered in neutral tones as she took her seat. "Apparently she's an old flame."

"Oh, yes, I remember Sin mentioning her." Charles nodded, looking after the departing couple with more interest. Cathy followed his gaze long enough to see the intent conversation, complete with soulful eye-flutterings from the black widow. Sin's back was to her, his head bent in an attitude of rapt attention. Cathy looked away.

"Well, I'm glad he's found someone," she managed to remark in a suitably languid tone. "I was afraid he'd feel bound to hang around with me, which, as you can imagine, is the last thing I wanted." Picking up her refilled champagne glass, she allowed herself another look over the rim of the glass. Just in time to see Joyce VanDeiler reach way up and wrap her black-clad arms around Sin's bent neck and press those bright red lips against his mouth. At that distance Cathy couldn't tell who had initiated the embrace, but then, she really didn't care, she told herself, setting the glass down with a tiny snap.

"I think I'll go up to bed," she said brightly. "I wouldn't want to be a fifth wheel."

"Don't leave yet, Cath," Meg begged, her dark eyes troubled. "I'm sure Sin will be right back. He couldn't have known that—that creature would show up. I'm sure he's just trying to get rid of her gracefully."

"Well, if I disappear then perhaps he won't feel that he has to get rid of her." Bending down to brush her sister's cheek, she left them with one more determined smile before vanishing out of the lounge.

The night was still and quiet, with the full moon bright above her head. *I seem to be making a habit of this,* she told herself grimly as she stepped onto the sandy beach. Silhouetted against one French door was a couple, sensuously entwined. The man was too short to be Sin, but the damage was done. Cathy yanked off her sandals, abandoning them in the sand, and started running down the beach, away from the noise and the laughter and the loving couples.

She ran until her heart pounded in her ears, throbbed in her chest, and her breath came in painful rasps, and still she ran. She fell once, skinning her knees in the wet sand, and then she was up and running again, as if Satan himself were after her. When she fell again by the rocks at the end of the small inlet she stayed down, letting her breath come in long, shuddering gasps into the wet sand, as hot, angry tears flowed down her face.

Slowly, slowly her sobbing breath quieted. The tears stopped their heated trail down her face, and her heart's rapid, frightened pounding slowed to a more reasonable rate. With her face still buried in the sand, she slowly became aware of her surroundings. The quiet *hush-hush* of the sea rolling onto the sand and the rocks. The smell of salt water and sea vegetation in the air, the burning of her skinned knees and the wet, sandy grit that bit through the clinging dress that was now irrevocably ruined. So much for the damned dress. It had hardly accomplished what she hoped it would.

There was another scent on the night breeze. For a moment Cathy thought it was her gardenia perfuming the air, then realized it was Sin's spicy aftershave. Did it still cling to her flesh, she wondered, after that all too brief embrace in their room? Or was it that interrupted dance?

Slowly, without moving her head, she opened one eye. A black-clad leg was beside her. Tilting her head, she looked up at Sin's motionless figure sitting in the sand next to her prone figure. His eyes were staring out at the ocean, as though looking for some sort of answer. She couldn't tell whether he had found it or not when he turned to meet her questioning gaze.

"Why did you leave?" His voice was low and beguiling on the night air. "Meg said you'd gone up to your room but I knew better. Particularly when I found these"—he held up her gold-strapped sandals—"on the beach."

"I wanted some fresh air," she said huskily, knowing full well how ridiculous the excuse sounded as she lay in the cool wet sand, her face wet with tears.

"You like running helter-skelter down a beach and then flinging yourself into the sand in tears?" he queried in soft mockery. "Mind you, I have noticed an unfortunate tendency to go racing off at the slightest provocation, but I would have thought—"

"I didn't fling myself onto the sand." She rolled over and sat up, brushing the clinging grains from her dampened front. "I tripped and fell." She lifted her skirt, took a brief peek at the graze which was now bleeding with a cheery profusion, and dropped the material back over it with a small shudder. "And I don't have a tendency to do any such thing," she added with a glare. "You bring it out in me."

"I'm sure I do." He brushed her hands away and lifted her skirt unnecessarily half way up her thigh, considering that the scrape was on her knee. "You did a good job with that," he remarked. "Come back with me and I'll get it cleaned up."

"It's nothing but a scratch," she muttered gracelessly. "I'll take care of it myself."

"I know that perfectly well. And I have no doubt you can clean it just as well by yourself. But I wanted to make sure you were all right."

"Did you promise Meg you'd check on me?" she shot back bitterly.

"Damn you, Cathy, are you never going to trust me?" His hand shot out and yanked her body across his, so that she was half sitting, half lying in his lap. She was so astounded she just sat there, without struggling, until his mouth came down on hers with a savage, bruising passion that seemed more of a punishment than a caress. And yet, curiously enough, Cathy responded to the savagery and unleashed desire as never before, opening her mouth beneath his and twining her arms around his neck, pulling his body closer to hers until she thought they might melt together.

Her tongue met his in a furious battle for dominance, until suddenly everything changed, and they were no longer waging a war but communicating needs and wants and desires in a silent sharing that reached beyond anything Cathy had ever known. And then Sin pulled his mouth away with a groan, burying his face against the curve of her neck.

"Damn you, Cathy," he said quietly, his breath coming rapidly. "And damn this dress, and most of all, damn Greg Danville." He looked up suddenly, and his eyes blazed into hers. "Tell me, Cathy, did Greg ever make you feel like this?" he demanded roughly. "Did he kiss you like this?" His mouth took hers, briefly, savagely. "And make you quiver in his arms like you do in mine?" He shook her. "Did he?"

Numbly she shook her head, and the smile of grim satisfaction that lit his face frightened her. "You're about as passive as a volcano," he muttered thickly, his mouth tracing hurried little kisses along her exposed collarbone. "And you're going back to your room right now, or I won't answer for the consequences."

Before she could protest he was on his feet, yanking her after him. "But I don't want..." she began, but his hand covered her mouth with surprising gentleness.

"Don't say it," he whispered. "You try a man too much, Cathy Whiteheart. And I can stand just so much at one time. You go on ahead to the hotel. I need to go for a long, soothing walk."

"But, Sin..." she tried again, but his hand covered her mouth again.

"Don't talk anymore, Cathy," he whispered.

"We'll talk for hours tomorrow. But unless you're willing to ask me to come back and make love to you, now, tonight, then don't say another word." He drew his hand slowly away, and his eyes burned down into hers wordlessly.

Once, twice, she opened her mouth to say the words that she wanted to say. But somehow the thought of coldbloodedly arranging her seduction at his too clever hands was more than she could manage. She wanted him to sweep her into his arms, drown her protests with his magical mouth, stifle any incipient revolt with those experienced hands and that lean, tightly muscled body. She wanted the decision taken from her, she realized, so that she wouldn't have to face the consequences of her action. And she wasn't ready for that, no matter how ready she was for the joining of their bodies.

A wry smile twisted his mouth beneath the mustache. "That's what I thought," he said with grim humor. Gently he leaned down and brushed his lips against her smooth forehead. "Go to bed, Cathy. I promise I won't be in until I can be trusted." Taking her shoulders in his strong hands, he turned her around and gave her a gentle push in the direction of the hotel.

She had no real choice but to go. Halfway back she turned to look at him. He was standing there, tall and stark on the moonlit beach, his face too distant to read his expression. It took all her self-control not to run back to him, barefoot across the wet sand. Resolutely she continued onward, and when she turned once more to look for him he was gone into the night.

Chapter Fifteen

Wearily she stretched her long, tanned legs in front of her and surveyed the slowly ascending sun. The coffee by her side had long since grown cold as the sun grew warmer, as cold as Cathy's hurt and fury. She had spent long hours waiting for him, lying in his bed wearing nothing but the gold chain about her slender waist, and still he hadn't come.

She dozed fitfully off and on, until her anger finally overcame her exhaustion, and she returned to her own bed, trying to shut out the image of Sin with his arms around that all too willing brunette. But still sleep eluded her, until she eventually moved from the bed to the tiny terrace, to sit in the comfortable chair and watch the sun rise over the deep blue ocean. She had already called the airline, and a ticket on the noon flight back to Washington awaited her. But first, she thought savagely, she would tell Sinclair

MacDonald exactly what she thought of him and his kisses and promises and faithlessness and...

A flash of reason inserted itself into her slowly boiling rage. What reason had he to be faithful to her? She was falling into the same trap that Charles and Meg had—assuming she had any claims on him simply because they were sharing a vacation and a room. And a few kisses. His eyes and his hands and his body had said he wanted her, and she hadn't answered. Was it any wonder he had sought more willing diversion for the night? Cathy's hands gripped the arms of the chair tightly as she stared out at the deserted beach. It was no wonder at all, especially considering how fickle men were. And she could only be grateful that he hadn't come in last night. If he hadn't found his...diversion, he would have returned to the room to find her waiting for him with open arms, all her defenses gone. And how would she have ever built them back up again, once he'd abandoned her?

The sound of the key in the lock alerted her to his return. The first runners were setting out along the beach below her, a white-jacketed waiter began setting up breakfast tables on the hotel's terrace restaurant. Cathy heard the door open and close, heard the steady measured tread of his footsteps heading toward her. She kept her sea-green gaze on the ocean in front of her, her back and shoulders rigid beneath the terry cloth robe.

"You aren't talking to me this morning?" His voice was low and caressing as he came to stand directly behind her.

"I have nothing to say," she said evenly. Unable to stand the suspense any longer, she tilted her back to stare at him over her shoulder. "Except to hope you had a pleasant night with Joyce."

He'd thrown his dinner jacket across the bed, and one hand was in the midst of unbuttoning the white shirt to expose his tanned chest dusted with curling brown hair. His face looked tired and somewhat surprised. Not the face of a man who had just spent a night of passion, but Cathy was in no mood to notice.

A slow, mocking smile spread across his weary face. "Why Catherine Whiteheart, I do believe you're jealous," he murmured. "Your eyes are like chips of green ice."

"Jealous?" she echoed with what she hoped was a suitably cynical laugh. "Jealous of you? Don't be absurd. I'm delighted you found someone more congenial to spend your nights with."

"Are you indeed?" He finished unbuttoning the shirt and sent it sailing onto the bed. "Is that why you spent at least part of the night in my bed?" he questioned silkily.

All hope of managing this with an icy dignity vanished. Leaping to her feet, she knocked over her chair and the half-full coffee cup. "Go to hell," she spat, storming past him to the bathroom.

His hand shot out and caught her wrist, whirling her around to face him. Instinctively she reached out and slapped him with all her strength. She scarcely had time to be appalled by her actions before he hit her back, hard.

Tears of pain and shock started in her huge green eyes, and she put her hand to her stinging cheek. "How dare you?" she whispered hoarsely.

There was not the slightest trace of compunction in his disturbing hazel eyes. "I thought you wanted to be treated as an equal," he shot back. "When an equal hits me I hit them back, whether they're a man or woman. I'm not about to let you go around demanding equality on your terms, and then turn into a helpless, clinging female when it suits you. You're going to have to expect to be hit when you slap someone."

"You're still a sexist," she fought back. "You pulled your punch. If you really looked on me as an equal you would have hit me harder."

His strong jaw tightened, and the exasperation that washed over his face was coupled with an awe inspiring rage. Flinging her wrist away in disgust, he turned and strode out onto the balcony, his broad back to her, as he took several deep, calming breaths. A moment later he turned back to her, a somewhat rueful expression on his face.

"You just made me lose my temper, Cathy," he said in a deceptively mild tone. "And I can be a hell of a lot more sexist than that. Come here, woman." Not waiting for her, he began to stalk her, a dangerous, determined glint in his eyes.

"No, Sin." She began to back away from him, panic and a strange anticipation causing her heart to pound furiously against her rib cage.

"No, Sin," he mocked. With his long legs he could move much faster than she could, and he caught up with her before she was halfway to the door. "How about, yes, Sin? Please, Sin? I'd like that, Sin?" His mouth was poised over hers as his arms held her pinned against his iron body. "Why do you fight me, Cathy? Why are you determined to think the worst of me? I spent the night on board the yacht because I didn't trust myself sharing a room with you. You sent me away last night. How was I to know you'd change your mind?"

"I—I didn't change my mind," she breathed, mesmerized by the mouth that was hovering just above hers.

"Then why did you sleep in my bed?" he queried again.

"Because I'm a fool," she whispered, closing her eyes as his mouth descended. Instead of the brutal assault she was somehow expecting, his mouth proved even more devastating. Light, clinging little kisses brushed across her tremulous lips, her cheeks, her nose, her eyelids. His mouth traced the still stinging imprint of his hand on her cheek, his lips nibbled on one pink earlobe, and then trailed down the slender column of her neck. Gentle, coaxing, teasing little kisses that left her trembling and completely demoralized. She slid her arms up his broad, naked back, pressing her body closer to his, her head flung back to give him better access to the sensitive hollow of her throat, the long blond hair a rippling curtain down her back. And then the world swung crazily about her as he scooped her up in his arms, holding her against his chest.

"Are you still a fool?" he whispered in her ear, his tongue tracing delicate little patterns as he moved toward the rumpled bed.

"Sin," she whispered, reaching up to entwine her hands in his soft brown curls. Her mouth met his, eagerly, hungrily as he laid her down on the soft bed, following her down, his body half covering hers, as the kiss deepened, her lips opening to meet his thrusting tongue as it explored the moist, sweet interior of her seeking mouth. "Yes," she murmured helplessly, as one hand cupped her full, straining breast, his thumb gently teasing the nipple until it stiffened against him. "Yes, yes, yes," she cried, as his hand slid down her thigh and began to lift the terry cloth robe.

The shrill ringing of the bedside telephone ripped them out of their dream of passion. With a precise expletive Sin rolled away from her, grabbing the phone before she could make a dive for it, and barking angrily, "Yes?"

As Cathy lay there, her robe up around her hips, her breath returning to normal, sanity began to edge back. Sin suddenly seemed to loom large and frightening beside her, his naked torso glistening with sweat, his broad shoulders tense with frustration and sudden anger.

"What?" he snapped into the telephone. "Are you sure?" He listened for another moment. "Well, Miss Whiteheart won't be needing the reservation after all. Thanks for your trouble, but her plans have changed. Yes, that's right." He slammed the receiver down, then turned back to Cathy's suddenly cowering figure.

Pulling herself upright, she managed to meet him glare for glare. "You had no right to do that," she said. "I have every intention of going back to Washington today."

"Why?" It was a simple enough question, but it was enough to break Cathy's tenuous self-control.

"Because I don't dare spend any more time with you!" she cried. "Can't you see what this is doing to me? I don't want to have a casual affair with you, Sin. I can't take that sort of thing. I'm not sophisticated enough to take and discard lovers like a change of clothes."

"You think it would be like that?" His voice was slow and deep and his face was unreadable.

"I know it would. You'd get tired of coping with

me, and some day, sooner or later, someone like Joyce Whatever-her-name-was will show up and you'll be off."

"You have a lot of faith in me," he said lightly, his hand gently smoothing a strand of hair away from her brow.

"Don't do that!" she cried desperately. "Leave me alone, please. If you don't ..." She let the sentence trail.

"If I don't?" he prompted, his voice deep and infinitely tender.

"If you don't," she continued weakly, "you'll only break my heart. And I couldn't bear it." Burying her face in her arms, she gave in to the tears that had racked her body the previous night. As she lay there she could feel his hazel eyes watching her, feel his warm, soothing presence beside her on the bed. But he made no move to comfort her, merely waiting until her sobs slowly died away.

"As I see it," Sin's voice said slowly, consideringly, "we have two options. Taking as given that I'm not about to let you go back to Washington, that is."

His reasonable tone was enough to make her raise her damp face curiously. "Why not?" she asked in a husky, tear-drenched voice.

He had moved to the other side of the bed and was leaning against the pillows. "Because I'm not," he replied shortly. "I want you here with me. So my options are simple: I can either kidnap you and keep you on my yacht, or"—he gave her a devastating smile—"we can get married."

The world seemed to spin about her. "I don't consider that amusing," she snapped.

"I wasn't planning on amusing you," he replied easily. "It's very simple to get a marriage license on St. Alphonse. We could be married this afternoon and then take off on *Tamlyn* for a honeymoon. Away from telephones and old flames and other distractions. What do you think?"

Cathy sat bolt upright, straightening the terry robe primly. "I think you're out of your mind," she announced firmly. "Why in the world would you want to marry me? You aren't in love with me." There was still enough foolishness in her that she hoped he might deny it.

He leaned back meditatively. "I don't know," he said dreamily. His eyes met hers suddenly, and Cathy felt a tightening in her stomach at the desire that blazed there. "I do know that I want to be with you. I want to make love to you, morning, noon, and night. You were made to be loved, Cathy, and you've spent far too much of your life celibate."

"That's not enough of a reason to get married," she said quietly. "Simple sexual attraction isn't enough. We could sleep together without getting married."

"Who said there was anything simple about sexual attraction?" he countered. "And there's more to it than sex, my love. I want to protect you, take care of you."

"I can take care of myself."

"Nonsense. You're far too vulnerable. How you could have gotten this far in life and still have remained so innocent is beyond me." He shook his head in amazement. "And though you're one of the toughest ladies I've ever met, you still need me."

"To protect me?" she repeated skeptically. "I don't think that's reason enough."

"What about this?" Before she could divine his intention, he had moved across the bed and caught her in his arms, his mouth crushing hers with a ruthless, demoralizing passion that was as soul-destroying as it was efficient. Part of her knew very well he was doing everything he could to turn her into a quivering mass of desire in the shortest amount of time. She knew it, and was helpless against it.

He moved his mouth a fraction of an inch away, keeping his arms securely around her. Not that she was about to try to struggle out of his embrace, she thought dizzily. "Marry me," he whispered.

"No." She shook her head, and his lips caught hers, gently teasing her into opening her mouth.

"Marry me," he said again, his tongue tracing her upper lip.

"No." The sound was definitely weaker. One

hand released its hold on her waist and cupped her soft breast.

"Marry me." He had moved her robe aside, and his tongue swirled around the rosy-tipped peak. A small, quiet moan of surrender emitted from the back of Cathy's throat.

"Yes," she whispered.

Chapter Sixteen

Cathy went through the wedding in a dream. She had dressed in the cream linen suit that Meg had rushed out and bought her, squeezed her feet into the matching shoes that were half a size too small, and stood in front of a tall black civil servant with her sister and Charles to one side and Sin, tall and somber and sinfully handsome, on the other. His voice had been low and deep and sure as he repeated the simple vows, Cathy's tone was a thin, reedy sound. *What am I doing,* she demanded of herself as she held out her hand and felt the thin gold band slip over her finger. *Am I out of my mind?*

Doubts had assailed her immediately. The moment she had whispered "yes" Sin had pulled away from her and rolled off the bed. "I feel like I've been waiting centuries," he'd said, shrugging into a forest-green polo shirt. "I can wait a few more hours. Besides, if we're going to get married this afternoon I have a thousand things to do."

Dropping a kiss on her bewildered forehead, he had vanished from the hotel room.

And this was the first time she had seen him since he had seduced her into agreeing to his crazy proposal. Standing tall and straight in front of the justice of the peace, with no chance for Cathy to come up with the hundred and one objections that had flooded her mind since he'd left her.

Even Meg had seemed strangely preoccupied, chattering at a breakneck speed that allowed Cathy no time at all for reflection or even confidences. All the while her dark eyes were troubled. Now as she stood next to her, holding the small bouquet of gardenias Sin had bought her, the troubled expression was still there. Out of the corner of her eye Cathy watched Charles reach out and pat Meg's hand in a reassuring gesture. He looked slightly grim around the mouth too, and Cathy's doubts increased tenfold.

Too late. "I now pronounce you man and wife," the justice announced. In a daze Cathy felt Sin's lips brush hers, followed by Charles and Meg, the doubts erased from their smiling countenances.

"I'll call Pops for you," Meg promised. "Leave it to me. He'll probably raise holy hell, but then, that's his usual style." She hugged her again, tears bright in her eyes. "God, I hope you're happy, Cath."

"Now, now, we don't need tears, darling," Charles chided genially, and Cathy couldn't tell if the geniality was forced or not. "I thought you loved romance."

"I just want to make sure Cathy's happy," Meg wailed, casting a fulminating glance at Sin's bland exterior. "And you'd damn well better know what you're doing," she informed her new brother-in-law.

Sin took this veiled threat in good part. "I do," he said simply, his arm moving to encircle Cathy's waist. She looked up at him, belated surprise and the return of her doubts clouding her expression.

"Well, shall we see the happy couple off, Meg?" Charles tried to inject a note of normalcy into the proceedings. "There's a bottle of champagne chilling on *Tamlyn*. I suggest we go toast the marriage and then let these two get off on their honeymoon."

"Sounds good," Sin agreed easily, taking her arm in a lightly possessive grip and guiding her toward the door. She tripped, and his grip tightened. "Are you all right?" The concern in his warm hazel eyes momentarily banished every doubt that had assailed her.

"I'm fine," she managed. "I'm not used to these shoes."

"It's bad luck for a bride to trip on her wedding day," Meg broke in before Sin could respond. "That's why they're carried over thresholds."

"I guess we didn't get off to a very good start then," Cathy said with a shaky laugh. Sin's body seemed curiously tense beside her, and she wished she could shake this sense of impending doom.

"We'll make up for it," Sin promised firmly, smiling down at her, and the warmth in his eyes melted her misgivings. When he looked at her like that she would do anything for him, even something as abysmally stupid and short-sighted as rushing into marriage.

Smiling back at him, she slipped out of her tight shoes and handed them to a bewildered Meg. "We need all the luck we can get," she murmured. "I don't want to tempt fate again."

And barefoot, she went with Sin out into the blazing tropical sunlight.

She had changed out of her linen dress and put on slim-fitting designer jeans and an oversized white cotton tunic that emphasized her tan while merely hinting at the ripe young curves beneath its billowing lines, and then joined her new husband on the deck as they sailed out of the harbor. They hadn't talked much, Sin being involved in the navigation of the yacht and Cathy being stricken with sudden, tongue-tied shyness. They had reached the tiny cove on the uninhabited island south of St. Alphonse in just under five hours, and right now the delicious odor of broiling steaks wafted in the open cabin door. Sin had insisted on taking care of dinner that night, brushing aside her offers of assistance with gentle determination. So that all she could do was sit barefoot on the bed she'd soon be sharing with her new husband and wonder if she'd gone out of her mind.

"Do you want some wine?" he called out cheerfully as he worked on the salad. "Or a drink of some sort?"

"No, thank you," she replied politely enough, leaning her head out of the cabin door for a moment. The small dimensions of the main cabin seemed dwarfed next to Sin's height. His back was to her, the faded jeans tight across his hips and clinging to his long, long legs. The western-style shirt hugged his broad shoulders, emphasizing the latent power they contained. With a sigh, Cathy moved back into the cabin, leaning up against the bulkhead. *Why?* she asked herself one more time. And with a sudden, blinding clarity, she knew.

You're in love with him, she accused herself silently. *Of all the stupid, idiotic, blind fools! You've been in love with him for days — weeks — and you never even noticed. No wonder you were so eager to be talked into a loveless marriage. Because on your side there was more than enough love. Stupid, stupid, stupid!*

And when had all this madness started? Once she realized the depth of her hopeless infatuation, the rest was easy. She'd been attracted from the first. But she'd been blinded by her lingering pain over Greg and a fear of new commitments, fighting the attraction with every ounce of her strength and stubborn will. But it had done her no good to fight.

She'd fallen in love with him the night he followed her out of the French restaurant in Georgetown and held her trembling, miserable body against his comforting warmth. And it had taken her another month to realize it! Well, she had never been noted for her wisdom in love. Witness Greg Danville.

Not a flicker of pain, she noticed with grim satisfaction. She was over him completely—at least loving Sin had accomplished that. But would the cure be worse than the illness? She had a wretched feeling that it might be.

"Dinner's ready." He was standing in the doorway, filling it completely. He even had to duck his head to move inside. "Are you all right?"

"Fine," she lied, looking at him with new eyes. "But I'm not really hungry."

"You should be." Taking her hand, he pulled her from the bunk and drew her out into the main cabin. "Have you eaten anything all day?"

"I had a sandwich sometime around noon." She failed to mention she'd left more than half of it behind on the plate. The little booth was set with white damask, silver candlesticks, and Waterford crystal wineglasses. A trace of humor penetrated her abstraction. "Do you usually travel with all this fancy stuff?" she queried, slipping into her place.

"Wedding present," he replied succinctly. "Meg didn't want us to use the same tin plates we'd used all the way down here." He placed a perfectly cooked steak in front of her with a flourish. The salad to her left was a work of art, with thinly sliced avocados spiraling around the outside. She looked up at him suspiciously.

"You told me you couldn't cook," she accused him after she took a tentative bite of the steak. It was perfect.

"When did I say that?" he demanded, surprised. "I love to cook."

"You told me that the first day I met you. When I said the men should fix lunch."

"Oh, that." He smiled wickedly, the corners of his eyes crinkling. "I only wanted to rescue you from an embarrassing situation. You were forced to admit you couldn't sail, and I didn't want you to feel any worse than you obviously already did."

"Rescue me?" she echoed. Despite the feeling of helplessness it connoted, the notion was very pleasant indeed. *Stop that,* she ordered herself sternly. *He's just got a Sir Galahad complex, and you're a damsel in distress. It's lucky he doesn't know how distressed you are, and all because of him.*

Surprisingly enough, she was hungry. After devouring her steak, she finished her salad, three rolls with butter, and almost half a bottle of champagne. Sin leaned back and watched her eat, with a light in his hazel eyes that was disturbingly tender. He was fast proving her undoing, Cathy realized hopelessly. And she knew without question that however miserable she'd been after Greg, it was nothing compared to the devastation Sin's eventual desertion would wreak.

"Penny for your thoughts?"

She forced herself to meet his eyes candidly. "I was wondering how long we'd be married," she said lightly, and had the dubious satisfaction of seeing the good humor vanish from his face.

"That's up to you," he said noncommittally.

"You'll let me go?"

A not entirely pleasant smile lit his tanned face. "Jumped at it, didn't you? No, I won't let you go. Not right now, at least."

"Then when?" she pursued it.

"Cathy." He leaned across the table and brushed her face with a gentle hand. "You agreed to marry me. Why all the doubts?"

She jumped like a frightened rabbit, pulling away from the caress as if burned. "Just nervous, I guess," she said shakily.

His eyes surveyed her for a long, speculative moment. "All right." He rose slowly to his full height, towering over her in the tiny confines of the cabin. Without another word he began clearing the table with an economy of movements. Cathy opened her mouth to offer to help him, then shut it again. If he did the dishes himself it would be longer before he turned his attention back to her. And she wasn't quite ready for the full force of that gaze.

Leaning her arms on the back of the bench seat, she stared out at the inky water beyond the porthole. "Do you mind if I go out on deck?" she asked suddenly.

Sin's eyebrows rose in surprise. "Of course not. As long as you don't jump overboard and try to swim for it. I wouldn't take kindly to a runaway bride."

"Where would I run to?" she asked in a low voice as she climbed the three short steps to the deck.

Once alone in the inky blackness, she took three long, deep breaths. The water was all around her, still and black, with a wide trail of moonlight cutting across it to the beach several hundred yards away. She could hear the quiet sounds of the water lapping on the hull, the soft breezes ruffling the palm trees on the shore and jiggling the hardware on the masts. Cathy sat cross-legged on the bench seat, drinking in the cool, sea-tanged night air, reveling in the deserted stillness, the calm and peace that surrounded her. For a moment she could almost forget the inexplicable mess she had landed herself in. Married to a man who didn't love her, a man whose presence sent her heart pounding and her pulses racing.

He moved so quietly she accepted his presence before she was completely aware of it. One strong, tanned hand reached out with a brandy snifter.

"I don't think—" Cathy began.

"Take it." The order was gently spoken, but an order nonetheless. "You need it. It's been a long, long day, and you didn't sleep much last night."

She took a tentative sip of the brandy, letting it burn its way down. He was so very close. She could feel the heat emanating from his body, smell the enticing male smell of him. Like a magnet she could feel her body being pulled toward his, and the idea panicked her.

"Let's go for a walk on the beach," she said suddenly. "It's such a pretty night and—"

"No." The word was quiet but inexorable.

Cathy swallowed once, twice, and took another sip of her brandy. "What about a swim, then? It looks like a lovely beach, and I love swimming at night."

"No." He leaned back against the cushions, his eyes glittering in the moonlit darkness.

"But it's early and I—"

"No." His voice was calm and implacable. "Finish your brandy, Cathy."

"I—I don't think I want it," she said nervously, getting to her feet and edging out of his way. She half expected him to catch her, but he made no move to impede her escape. "I think I'll go below and—and find something to read. I'm not at all tired, and reading always helps me sleep." The words came out breathlessly and far too fast. Sin had the indecency to laugh at her lame excuse, but he let her go without moving.

Chapter Seventeen

The main cabin was no escape, and the small room she would soon have to share with Sin was even worse. Cathy whirled about her in panic, wishing now she *had* jumped overboard. She didn't want ... she couldn't ...

Sin moved slowly down the steps, lithe and graceful as a jungle cat, despite his height. Placing the brandy snifters on the tiny counter, he turned to face her in the small confines of the cabin. There was a look of intractable purpose in his face as he moved slowly toward her.

"No, Sin," she gasped, backing away. But in that small room there wasn't much space to back into.

"Yes, Sin," he corrected gently. "Yes, indeed, Sin. Yes, please, Sin." He reached out and caught her by the retreating shoulders, his hands warm and firm and inflexible. "Don't run anymore, Cathy," he whispered, drawing her slowly toward him. His hands ran up her shoulders to her neck, cupping her face, and his eyes burned down into her frightened green ones. Slowly, agonizingly slowly, his mouth descended to capture hers, his lips moving against hers in a sensual appeal. The only parts of his body touching hers were his mouth on hers and the hands holding her throat, the thumbs stroking along the side of her neck slowly, sensuously, as his tongue explored the wet, hungry interior of her mouth. Cathy's hands were at her side, her fists clenched, and she willed herself to resist the practiced seduction of that experienced mouth. But Sin had all the time and patience in the world, teasing, enticing, seducing her with his tongue, until her arms slid around his waist of their own volition, pulling him closer against her yearning body.

His mouth left hers to bury in her neck, the lips nibbling at the sensitive cord above her collar. "Say it, Cathy," he whispered against her heated flesh. "Say that you want me."

She shook her head helplessly. "No," she whispered. The hand on her neck slid back to her shoulders, and she felt herself pushed a few inches away. It seemed like miles, when all she wanted to do was bury herself against his leanly muscled strength.

"No?" he echoed, his eyes blazing, his voice soft but implacable. "Do you really mean that?"

They stared at each other for a long, tension filled moment. And Cathy knew that this was her last chance. All she had to do was tell him no, one more time, and she would never have to worry about being further enthralled by the strange power he had over her. One word and he would release her forever.

"Answer me, Cathy," he said, and his voice was fire and ice. "Do you mean that?"

"No," she whispered. "I mean, yes. I mean . . ." She stumbled helplessly to a halt. And still he waited, unwilling to help her. She had to cross that last bridge alone.

Reaching up, she covered his hands with hers, pressing them against her shoulders. "Yes, Sin," she said, her voice husky. "I want you."

A slow smile spread across his face. "You've got me," he said simply. A moment later one arm had slid under her knees and she was in his arms, held high against his chest with effortless ease. "Lady, you've got me for as long as you want me," he promised, and his mouth found hers again as he carried her into the front cabin, kicking the door shut behind them.

Moonlight was streaming in the open hatch over their heads, casting silver shadows on the wide berth as he gently laid her down, his body following hers with pantherlike grace.

"You aren't still afraid of me, are you, Cathy?" he whispered, staring down at her.

She gazed up at the bronzed, unreadable features poised above her, and she shook her head, the last of her misgivings vanishing. She loved him and wanted him, had loved and wanted him for what seemed an eternity. And now, for at least a time, he was hers. She smiled up at him tremulously, raising a tentative hand to the buttons of his shirt. He lay there on his side, motionless, his eyes burning into hers, as she fumbled with the final button of his shirt and slid her hand across the heated flesh of his chest. The skin was smooth and muscled beneath the light layer of curls, and Cathy sighed.

"To think I didn't use to like men with hair on their chests," she murmured dreamily, raising her other hand to slip the shirt off his broad shoulders. He moved a bit to help her, then rolled back on his side, one hand possessively on her slender hip, an amused smile lighting his eyes as she discovered the wonders of his body.

Slowly she let her hand trail across his flat stomach, until, on impulse, she leaned down and buried her mouth against his chest. She could feel his heart pounding against her lips, slow, heated beats that betrayed his need for her. Smiling against his flesh, she slid her hand up his smoothly muscled back, her sensitive fingers kneading his hungry skin with soft, sure strokes. His breath was coming more rapidly now, ruffling her silken hair as she moved her mouth across the muscled planes of his stomach and up his chest. Her hand trailed back across his stomach, drifted lower to the belt of his jeans, and then jerked back, her courage finally failing her.

"Coward," he laughed softly in her ear, catching her reticent hand and moving it lower. She let out a small gasp of surprise, her widened eyes meeting his. "Is that all the exploring you're going to indulge in, darling?" he whispered against her ear, his tongue tracing the delicate lines. "There's a great deal more of me to discover." His hand reached up to cup her chin, his thumb gently stroking her trembling lips.

Moving over, he replaced his thumb with his lips, kissing her slowly, deeply, with a languorous passion that set the fires in her loins burning more fiercely. She was barely aware of his hand undoing the buttons of her shirt, pulling back the cottony material and dispensing with the front clasp of her lacy bra with practiced ease, his hand caressing one soft, aching breast possessively, his sensitive fingertips gently stroking the tender nipple.

"Oh, God," he breathed suddenly, his voice husky with passion. "I can't stand these damned clothes any longer!" With an impatience that bordered on savagery he unzipped her jeans and stripped them from her body, tossing them on the floor with her shirt and bra. His jeans followed, and then there was nothing separating them but their own determination to wring every last, lengthy ounce of pleasure from a moment long denied.

His lips found one soft breast in the moonlight, his tongue flickering across the suddenly rigid nipple as Cathy moaned, her fingers digging into his shoulders. His hand trailed up her slender thigh, softly tantalizingly, until he reached the center of her soul-destroying need. She jerked away, startled, but his sure, gentle stroking first calmed, then overwhelmed her. She arched her hips against his hand, little whimpers of desire echoing from the back of her throat. The burning fires had turned into a conflagration, one that threatened to destroy her. Her body trembled and shook all over with the desperation of her need, a need she had never known before. Sin pulled his mouth reluctantly away from her breast and trailed small, damp kisses across her collarbone, all the while his clever, clever hands were driving her to the edge of madness and beyond.

"Sin," she gasped, her nails digging into his flesh. "Please, Sin. Oh, please..." she moaned, moving her head back and forth in the extremity of her need.

His hands left her, catching her head and holding it still as his eyes bored down into hers. "Are you ready so soon?" he whispered sweetly against her mouth. "I was expecting to have to coax and reassure you for hours yet."

"Don't...tease me," she gasped.

A slow, tender smile curved his mouth. "Never, my sweet." And, setting his hungry mouth on hers, he moved over and covered her body with his, joining them at last in that final embrace, swift and sure and deep. They moved together in perfect union, a masterful blend of mind, body, and spirit, until the blazing conflagration engulfed them both in a fiery holocaust that left them, weak but replete, to struggle upward, phoenixlike, from the ashes of their fulfillment.

Sin reached out a tender hand to brush the hair away from her flushed, sweat-dampened face. The cool wetness of tears caught his fingers, and very tenderly he leaned over and kissed them away.

"Sin, I . . ." His hand covered her mouth before she could tell him, before she could say that she loved him.

"Not now," he whispered, his warm breath tickling her ear. "Don't tell me now." He pulled her exhausted body against his, spoon-fashion, cradling her against his taut, sweat-drenched leanness. And before she had time to wonder why he would stop what would surely have been a very satisfying confession, sleep claimed her, leaving her wrapped in her lover's arms and at peace with the world.

Cathy woke, slowly at first, the thoughts and feelings and images drifting lazily through her sleep-fogged brain. All along her left side was warmth and comfort, and a heavy weight was pressing around her middle, a weight she slowly realized was Sin MacDonald's arm. One large hand was cupping her breast, and despite the even rise and fall of his breathing she knew he was more than aware of her. She lay very still, reveling in the feel of his strong, lean body against hers.

"Good morning," his voice rumbled in her ear, sounding sleepy, smug, and satisfied. As indeed, she herself was. "How long have you been awake?" He stretched beside her, rubbing his body against hers slowly and sensually.

"About half an hour," she replied honestly, snuggling back against him. "I felt too happy to sleep."

His arm tightened around her, and she felt her body being drawn slowly back down onto the bed. He leaned over her, pressing her against the soft mattress, and the look on his face was tender, and, even if he wouldn't put the word to it, loving. "Then you've only had a total of about an hour's sleep," he said with a lascivious grin. "Aren't you tired? You certainly should be after the workout you gave me last night."

"The workout I gave *you*?" she shrieked, albeit softly. "I'll have you know, Sin MacDonald, that I was sound asleep when you ... when we ..."

His grin broadened. "You can still blush," he marveled. "Not that I'm surprised—if anything could make you blush, that infamous 'when we ... when you ...' should. And I'll have you know, Cathy MacDonald, that I was sound asleep the time before, when you ... when we ..."

"You're incorrigible," she said crossly, trailing her hand up his tautly muscled arm. "And who says I don't want to keep my maiden name?" she added teasingly.

She had the dubious satisfaction of seeing his

hazel eyes turn fiery with rage. Covering the lower half of her body with his stronger one, he held her captive as his hand cupped her mutinous face. "*I* say," he informed her huskily. "That five-minute ceremony made us one, a unit, and I want us to stay that way. In name, in spirit, and"—he let his hips bump against hers suggestively—"in body."

Her eyes widened in shocked recognition. "Good heavens, Sin. Not again," she breathed, her eyes alight as she lifted her mouth for his possession.

He kissed her long and deep, with a savagery that alarmed and excited her. "Is that a protest?" he murmured hoarsely against her throat.

"Hm-mn," she denied with a low guttural noise, a purr of pleasure as her tired body responded once more to his practiced caresses. "Merely an expression of awed wonder." And sliding her deft hands down his lean torso, she met his passion fully, exploding within moments of him as they reached the apex of their perfect desire. And once more they slept.

"You know, you don't really need to wear that," Sin said lazily as he stretched out on the bunk beside the small kitchen. He caught hold of the short, velour wrapper she'd appropriated from him as she tried to find her way about the pocket-sized galley. It fell to just below her knees, and must have been barely decent on Sin's lengthy frame, she thought wistfully.

"Don't mess with the chef," she ordered sternly, twitching the robe out of his grasping fingers. "If you want coffee you have to let me get to it." She fumbled with the automatic coffeemaker, mastering its intricacies with her usual difficulty with mechanical objects.

His hazel eyes were half-closed as he surveyed her lithe form, and Cathy knew perfectly well that his imagination was stripping away the robe with devastating accuracy. She could feel the color rising, and she forced herself to turn and survey him with the same sensual directness. Leaning against the counter, she let her hungry eyes roam over his tanned, muscular body. From the long, long legs, the trim hips and lean buttocks encased in the scantiest excuse for underwear Cathy had ever seen, the flat stomach and broad, hair-fringed chest that she had wept and moaned and laughed into last night. *And this morning,* she added silently. To the broad shoulders, strong arms, and diabolically clever hands that seemed instinctively to know what part of her needed to be touched, with just the right amount of gentleness or force. And the hazel eyes that looked so tenderly into hers, the mouth that had taught her things she had scarcely known existed. All in all it was a very potent package, she realized with a small blissful sigh.

The tiny laugh lines around his eyes crinkled in amusement. "I'd ask you what you were thinking but I'm sure I'd be shocked out of my mind." He accepted the coffee she offered, never taking his eyes off her. "And I don't see why I have to wear these." He plucked at the briefs. "I'll allow you your modesty, but when there's no one around for miles and miles..."

"You have to wear them," she said, sitting down cross-legged beside him and sipping at her rich black coffee, "because I find you far too distracting without them. It's hard enough to concentrate on cooking as it is. What do you want for dinner?"

His eyes roamed lazily over her. 'You," he said, pulling her down to lie against his broad, hard chest without spilling a drop of her coffee.

"I think you're going to need something a bit more substantial if we're going to keep on at the pace we've started," she said, sighing happily. She let one hand trail intimately across his stomach, listening to his stifled groan of pleasure with a smile as she snuggled closer against his chest. She took another sip of her coffee. "Speaking of food—you know what the trouble with you is?"

His arms tightened companionably around her slender form, one hand dipping into the robe to touch her breast. "No, tell me. What is the trouble with me?" he demanded lazily, showering small, unhurried kisses in her cloud of silver-blond hair.

She moved her head to look down at him mischievously. "You're like Chinese food," she explained in dulcet tones. "Very satisfying at the time, but a half an hour later I'm hungry again."

A shout of laughter greeted her impish remark. Taking the half-empty coffee cup from her hand, he placed it on the table beside his, then stretched back, taking her with him, so that her slender, half-clad form was stretched out on top of his lean, strong body. It was a dizzying feeling, with his warm flesh and hardening desire beneath her, waiting for her. With a sigh she buried her head against his chest, nestling against the soft cushion of hair as his hands reached beneath her robe.

"All I can say," he sarcastically murmured in her ear, "is that it's a lucky thing you're frigid. God knows what I'd do with you if you actually liked to make love." His hips, magically divested of the restraining briefs, reached up to meet hers, as her whole body tensed.

"What's the matter?" His voice was soft and patient, unlike his passion-stirred body.

She tried to pull away from him, but his hands sensed her withdrawal and reached up to stop her, holding her frailness against him.

"It's just..." Her words faded for a moment, then strengthened. "You reminded me of something I'd rather forget."

"Greg Danville," he supplied in a short, angry voice. At her reluctant nod, his grip tightened. "Listen, Cathy," he said in a surprisingly stern tone, "Greg existed. You can't wipe him out of your life, forget that you ever knew him or that he ever hurt you. It happened. But it's over, long over. And it has nothing to do with you and me, and what we have together. Nothing at all. Is that understood?'' Despite the sternness there was a gentleness in his eyes and the hands that held her captive against his still fully aroused body. "Is it?" he demanded again.

And strangely enough, it was true. Greg Danville was out of her life, never to be heard from again. He had nothing to do with her and Sin, nothing whatsoever. She managed a smile, tentative at first, then widening with real delight. "Yes, sir," she said sweetly. And then with dizzying force he turned her over onto the bunk, covering her body with his ardent one. And Greg Danville vanished completely in a torrent of desire.

Chapter Eighteen

Cathy sat on the deck, soaking up the hot, Caribbean sun with truly hedonistic fervor. Her body was turning a lovely golden brown, setting off the thin gold chain with its perfect emerald, and she felt warm, full, and completely satiated. She reached out to touch the emerald, which served as a sort of talisman for her. Any time she began to doubt what had happened to her during the past weeks, and particularly the past two days since she married Sinclair MacDonald, she would reach for the chain through her clothing or, more frequently, on her naked body, and touch it. For good luck, or to remind herself that it was real. She wasn't sure which—maybe a little bit of both. Her eyes trailed across the deck to Sin's lean frame. He was hunched over some piece of equipment, his face intent beneath the sunglasses, his tanned body, clad only in the briefest of denim cutoffs, glistening with the sun and a light film of sweat.

"I hated to leave that island," Cathy said dreamily. "Everything was perfect there. The water, the sun, the privacy."

He looked up and smiled at her, easily, casually, the very naturalness of it incredibly sexy. "I hated to leave it too," he replied, squinting out at the horizon. "But we need supplies, and Martin's Head is the closest place I know. We can sail right back."

"No, I don't think so," she sighed. "For some reason I'm afraid it will have vanished if we try to find it again. You don't even know what island it is, do you?"

"Hey, I'm not that bad a navigator. I can find it again," he protested. "Or maybe we can find another island."

She turned to peer up at him in the brilliant sunlight. "That would be nice," she sighed. "We may never run out of islands at this rate."

He seemed to hesitate, on the verge of saying something and then obviously thought better of it. He returned his attention to the instrument in his hand, his fingers as dexterous on the intricate machinery as they were on her responsive body.

"What were you about to say?" she questioned curiously, pulling herself to a sitting position and retying the straps to her bikini behind her neck.

"Was I about to say something?" he murmured vaguely. "Can't remember what."

"Maybe it was something about when we have to go back," she prodded, a flicker of nervousness racing along her veins. "You know," she added with an uneasy laugh, "I don't really know what you do for a living."

There was no mistaking the wariness in his body. She knew every inch of it far too well by that time to miss his reaction. "Sure you do," he said easily, too easily. "I told you before, I'm a consultant."

"But for whom?" she persisted. "Oh, I remember. That Joyce-woman said you own your own company. Is that why you're able to just disappear on your honeymoon without telling anyone?"

He put the piece of machinery down, turning to stare at her with lazy charm. "Why the cross-examination, Cathy?" he inquired evenly. "I'm more than happy to tell you anything you want to know."

"Even about Joyce?" she dared to ask.

"Even about Joyce," he agreed. "Though I can't imagine why you'd want to know. I never pretended to be a monk before I met you, sweetheart. Joyce and I were ... close at one time."

"You mean you were lovers," she said flatly, miserably aware of how bitchy she sounded.

"Yes." His answer was unequivocal.

"And how many others?"

The last trace of a smile was wiped from his face. "I lost count," he snapped, crossing the small section of deck to kneel down beside her. "What the hell is wrong with you, Cathy?" he demanded roughly, pulling her unresisting body into his arms with an anger that was oddly reassuring.

"I'm sorry," she said meekly against his firmly muscled chest. "I guess I'm just on edge. I'm afraid that everything is going to end in disaster since we've left the island. Can't we go back?" she pleaded.

Tenderly he pushed the hair from her face, a crooked smile that didn't belie his own misgivings playing about his mobile mouth. "We'd starve to death, baby," he said softly. "Don't be so gloomy. We'll stop at the store on Martin's Head, be there for a total of fifteen minutes and then be off. You can do the shopping while I get fresh water and fuel on board. And then we'll be miles away again, where no one can get to us. How does that sound?"

His hand was gently stroking the slender curve of her waist as he held her against his broad, firm chest. He smelled of suntan oil and sun-heated flesh, a potent combination that stirred her senses. She could feel the tension draining out of her as she wondered if she'd ever tire of his magnificent body.

"It sounds heavenly," she sighed. But still, in the back of her mind, the misgivings remained.

Martin's Head was smaller than she had imagined, and the tiny store looked dark and depressing. Leaving Sin at the dock, haggling with a cheerful-looking pirate, she made her way up the winding path to the small store, determined to complete her business and be gone as quickly as possible. It was the sight of the telephone booth that diverted her intentions.

The only cloud on her blissful horizon the last few days was the lack of word from her father. Meg had promised to call him from St. Alphonse with the news of Cathy's precipitous wedding, but the absence of her father's good wishes suddenly overwhelmed her. On impulse she abandoned her shopping for the telephone, her heart pounding with sudden excitement and happiness. She couldn't wait to tell Pops about Sin. They'd like each other, she knew they would. And Pops would hardly object—he'd been wanting her to get married for years. While he was secretly very proud of her insistence on working at the day-care center, he still held to the antiquated notion that a woman couldn't be happy unless he had a husband and children on the way. Cathy put a tentative hand on her flat belly as she waited for the call to go through, surprised to find that she was beginning to agree with him. The thought that she might be carrying Sin's child was infinitely precious to her.

"Well, well, if it isn't my little sister Cathy," Travis's hateful voice drawled at the other end of the surprisingly good connection. "We hadn't expected to hear from you for ages. How's the honeymoon? Enjoying your stalwart private eye?

Your father was fit to be tied, you know. Security is one thing, but this is carrying it a bit too far, don't you think?''

"What in the world are you talking about, Travis?" Cathy demanded. The connection was crystal clear, but Travis's conversation was definitely full of static. "Can I speak to Pops?"

"Oh, you most assuredly can. There's no way I can stop him—" His sentence ended in the middle, and then her father was on the phone, breathing heavily.

"It's about time you called," he said gruffly. "Where the hell are you?"

"On a small island called Martin's Head," she replied in bewilderment. "Didn't Meg call you? I'm married. To a—"

"Your idiot sister most certainly did call me. And I know Sin MacDonald a hell of a lot better than you do. I hired him."

Slowly, her body began to go numb. Starting at her toes, and working its way slowly upward through her loins and her heart, until the only part of her that still worked was her brain. "You what?" she echoed.

"I hired him. Haven't you ever heard of Mac-Donald and Anderson?" he snapped.

"They're your security firm," she replied vaguely. "But what . . . ?"

"Sinclair MacDonald is the president of Mac-Donald and Anderson. He's worked for me for years, on special projects and the like."

There was a long silence. "The latest of which is me?" she questioned finally in a dead voice.

Her deathly reaction finally penetrated the miles of telephone cable to her father. "No, don't take it like that, honey. You were in danger. That psycho you hooked yourself up with last spring has been trying to extort money from me. Said he'd wreck your life if I didn't turn over a very large sum of money to him. I remember how much you seemed to love the guy—I thought he could do it. So I hired Sin MacDonald to get you out of the country and out of Danville's way till we could take care of him."

"I see." She was amazed at how calm her voice sounded. "And did Meg and Charles have anything to do with this?"

"Well, of course." Her father had the grace to sound somewhat sheepish. "How else could we have managed it? You weren't about to fall for him on your own. But honey, listen, it's all over. We've got Danville dead to rights. We've gotten a restraining order, and if he comes anywhere near you he'll be slapped in jail so fast his head will spin. Even if we don't make the charges stick he won't ever try to pull a stunt like this one again."

"Great."

"So you can come home, honey. If that was a real marriage Sin arranged we can manage a speedy annulment. But I sure as hell can't figure out why he went that far."

"I was about to fly back home," Cathy said

flatly. "He probably thought marrying me was the only way to stop me. He's a very thorough man, Mr. Sinclair MacDonald."

"He is indeed," her father agreed jovially, his voice plummy with satisfaction. "In that case I'm sure the marriage isn't legal. No problem, then. You just catch the first plane home and we'll put all this behind us. Meg and Charles are already back. You can tell Sin for me there'll be a bonus for him. Not that he needs one, at the prices I pay him already."

"I'll be sure to tell him. I'll be home tomorrow."

"That long?" Brandon Whiteheart was displeased.

"It'll take a while to get to an island with an airport. I won't take any longer than I have to—" The phone was removed from her hand with inexorable force. Turning to look up at her husband's face, she let go, keeping her own face carefully blank.

"It's your boss," she said politely, and turning her back on him, she walked back to the boat.

Chapter Nineteen

It didn't take her long to throw her clothes into the duffel bag she'd brought along. Sin had insisted she wouldn't need many clothes on her honeymoon, an insistence time had borne out. Cathy was cold and dry-eyed, an icy film covering her heart and soul. Even the feel of Sin's heavy footsteps climbing onto the boat failed to break through her iron control, although her senses told her when he entered the cabin on silent feet.

"How long will it take to get to St. Alphonse?" She kept her back to him and her voice cool and composed.

"Eight or ten hours, probably." His voice matched hers for coolness. "We'd have to make it under power—there's not a breath of wind."

"Then we can make it there by tonight?" She spent more time and attention folding a pair of jeans than she had taken with the entire sum of her other clothing.

"By tomorrow. I'm not about to spend all night

sailing, and it's already five o'clock. We wouldn't be in till three or four in the morning. It can wait."

She steeled herself to turn and meet his gaze. His face was completely expressionless in the dim confines of the cabin, and it was with an overwhelming effort that Cathy stopped herself from screaming at him. "Is there an island closer that has an airport?" she questioned politely.

"St. Alphonse is the nearest one. Are you going home?" The question was asked in a tone of polite disinterest, a tone that Cathy matched perfectly.

"As soon as I possibly can."

He stared down at her for a long, silent moment. She could see a tiny muscle working in his strong jaw, the only sign that her new-found knowledge affected him in the slightest.

"In that case," he said flatly, "I suppose we should get under way. There are still a few good hours of sunlight left." Without another word he turned and left her alone in the cabin.

She looked down at the wide bed they had shared, and an involuntary moan of pain issued from the back of her throat. She clamped her teeth shut on it, shoving the neatly folded jeans into the duffel bag and zipping it shut. The next twenty-four hours would take a century to pass, she thought wearily as she sat cross-legged on the bed. *And I won't cry. If I can just keep away from him I'll make it through. As long as I don't have to spend any more time with his lying eyes, that damnable smile that promised love and tenderness.*

But he never told you he loved you, she reminded herself, determined to be fair. *He may have lied about everything else, but he never told that final, unforgivable lie. Damn it, don't cry,* she threatened herself, pinching her leg fiercely to stop the treacherous weakening. *Because once you start crying,* she warned herself, *you won't ever stop.*

The hours passed at a snail's pace, even more slowly than Cathy had anticipated. At one point the faint aroma of chicken soup wafted through the tightly shut door, followed by a short, staccato knock.

"Do you want anything to eat?" Sin's voice was cool and composed, entirely in control of the situation, apparently.

And why did the sound of his deep voice still have the power to melt her bones, after his lies and betrayal? "Nothing," she snapped, more fiercely than she had intended. His footsteps moved away, leaving her once more to fight off the misery that threatened to overwhelm her. She stayed on the bunk, curled up in a tight, dry-eyed ball of despair behind her locked door, hidden away, her privacy the only solace she could find on that tiny, floating hell.

When she awoke it was just past midnight, according to the luminous dial of the thin gold watch Sin had left by the bed. The boat was dark and silent—sometime during the last few hours Sin must have dropped anchor. Not a sound issued from the main cabin, nothing to hint that she wasn't alone on the boat. But she knew far too well that she shared the boat, and the last thing in the world she wanted was to risk waking her—her father's hired man. No matter how lonely the bed suddenly seemed.

Nature, however, had other ideas. The only bathroom on the boat was just outside the tightly locked door, and it soon became apparent that she would have to leave the safety of her refuge. She would simply have to trust to a not very kind fate that Sin would be sound asleep and not notice her tiptoeing across the cabin.

There was no sign of him as she slipped out of the master cabin and into the confines of the head. Breathing a sigh of relief, she decided to allow herself the luxury of brushing her teeth and washing her face. The haunted green eyes that stared back at her out of the curtain of silver-blond hair had an eerie familiarity. She had spent the summer just like this. She recovered from Greg Danville; why did she have the depressing conviction that Sin MacDonald would be a great deal harder to forget? She had always known it.

Tears began to form in the green eyes, and she quickly splashed cold water in them. Sliding back the bathroom door, she started out into the main cabin, only to run smack into Sin's large, immovable body.

There was a quick, indrawn gasp, before Cathy jumped back. Or tried to. His large, strong hands caught her shoulders in an iron grip, holding her rigidly a few inches from him. From the glitter in his eyes she could tell he was in a deep, towering rage, from his rapid breath that fanned her face she could detect the faint trace of brandy. The look of the panther was back, overpowering in its threat of danger and savagery. It was all Cathy could do to stop from quailing before the intensity in his strongly marked face.

"Are you going to talk to me?" he demanded, all trace of composure gone. He shook her once, hard. "Are you? Or are you going to spend the rest of the time sulking in that damned cabin?"

"I'm going to spend the rest of the time sulking in that damned cabin," she shot back, her own coolness vanished in the face of his attack. "We have nothing to say to each other." She struggled helplessly. "And get your hands off me."

Her heart was pounding with a mixture of fear, anger, and a desire that nothing could destroy, not even the full knowledge that he had tricked her. *Maybe that's what love is,* she thought miserably, still glaring up into his angry eyes. *A wanting that nothing can destroy.* And some part of her wanted to reach up and smooth his tumbled hair out of his flushed face, to reassure him — to apologize, of all things! And what did she have to apologize for? He was the one who had lied and cheated, who trapped her with her own needs. She clenched her fists to keep that soothing hand from moving upward of its own volition.

The fingers that clenched her shoulders loosened somewhat, to slide down her bare arms. "Maybe you're right," he said slowly, his eyes hooded. "Maybe we do have nothing to say to each other. And maybe you *should* spend the rest of the time in your cabin. With me," he added crudely. "Because I sure as hell am not going to take my hands off you." With a suddenness that threw her off balance he yanked her into his arms, so that she fell against his broad, hard chest. Her arms were trapped between them as his mouth came down on hers with punishing savagery. Desperately she fought him, keeping her mouth tightly shut against his insistent, probing tongue, as his hands slid down her arched back and cupped her firm buttocks, pressing her up against his angry male desire. And then the room swung crazily around as he scooped her slight body up and carried her back into the cabin, dropping her unceremoniously on the bunk.

"Don't you dare do this!" she spat at him as he stripped her thin cotton knit shirt over her head with deadly efficiency. "Haven't you humiliated me enough?" His deft hands dispensed with her tight jeans, brushing aside her furious fists. A moment later he was naked in the bed beside her, her wrists held above her head in a grip of iron clothed in velvet. His other hand caught her chin and held it still, his eyes burning down into hers for a long, breathless moment.

"I'm not going to rape you, Cathy," he said

huskily. "Because I know too well how to make you want me. You're my wife, dammit. And even if it's only for one more night, I intend to be your husband." And his mouth dropped down to take possession of hers, this time with none of the savagery that had marked his rage in the outer cabin, but with a slow, insinuating thoroughness that had her shuddering with a tightly controlled longing. His mouth trailed tiny, passionate kisses across her neck, down her collarbone, his lips capturing one nipple as it swelled in response. His callused hand traveled down the firmness of her flat belly, stroking the smooth, soft skin as his fingers moved ever closer to that aching, secret part of her that already knew him so well. And then his hand moved up, away, to stroke the outline of her hip, her waist, all the while his mouth concentrating on the upper half of her body, his lips teasing, tantalizing, until her slender frame squirmed with a longing she could no longer deny.

Once more his hand trailed down her body, to dance lightly across her stomach, down to her thighs, and then away. Wordlessly she arched her body, vainly trying to reach his dilatory hand. He moved up and kissed her again, and this time she opened her mouth eagerly to him, her tongue meeting his in a tiny duel of passion that promised no victor and no vanquished. And then as a reward his hand moved back, to the very center of her longing, stroking her with a knowledge that scorched her even as it brought her to the edge of oblivion.

Finally he released her wrists, levering his body across hers. She should push him away, she told herself dazedly, wrapping her arms tightly around him as her hips pushed mutely against his hand.

"Say it," he whispered in her ear, his breath hot on her yearning flesh. "Tell me you want me."

She shook her head, clamping her strong white teeth down on her lips that would have told him anything he wanted. Abruptly his hand left her.

"No," she whispered, tears streaming down her pale face unbidden, the final vestiges of control vanishing. "No," she repeated, refusing to give him his last victory. He knew as well as she did how much she wanted him; she wouldn't give him the final triumph of begging him.

He stared down into her tear-drenched face for a long, unfathomable moment, and in the darkness his face was anguished. And then his mouth caught hers as he completed their union, his body taking hers with a mastery that left him as much a slave as she was.

Helplessly she fought the spasms that washed over her, the feel of his strong, powerful body above her, between her, inside her. But it was a useless struggle, one Sin knew he would win long before he carried her into the cabin. Wave after wave of ecstasy washed over her, and dimly she could hear a voice, *her* voice, sobbing in fulfillment.

It seemed a long time later that he lifted his spent body away from hers. Gentle hands reached up to smooth her face, and his head bent low to capture her lips. She turned her face abruptly away, her eyes shut tight, the tears still streaming down her flushed face. She could feel him hesitate above her, and the thumbs kept stroking her teardrenched cheeks.

"Cathy," he said gently, his voice tender.

"Go away," she grated, her body stiff in his arms. "Haven't you done enough?" She opened her eyes to stare at him with unalloyed hatred. "I'll never forgive you for that! Never!" Her voice was low and bitter, and there was no doubt that she meant what she said.

Slowly his arms released her, the loving tenderness wiped from his face, leaving it blank and cold once more. "No," he said wearily, sitting up and reaching for his discarded jeans, "I don't suppose you ever will." And a moment later he was gone, closing the door silently behind him.

The engines throbbed to life. He was taking her back, she realized numbly. Traveling at night had suddenly lost its lack of appeal. Turning her face into the pillow, Cathy wept.

Chapter Twenty

Cathy pressed her foot down on the accelerator, speeding along the Virginia countryside as if the devil himself were after her. When, in fact, he'd abdicated, leaving her to wake, alone and bereft, on the docked ship on the busy island of St. Alphonse. There had been no sign of him as she hastily scrambled into her clothes, and she hadn't wasted time looking for him. At the last moment, pulling the thin cotton shirt over her head, she noticed the gold chain that still circled her waist. With a savage yank she ripped it off, breaking the delicate links. Throwing it on the rumpled bed, she pulled at her gold wedding band, intending that it should follow suit. But the wedding ring stuck. Desperately she pulled at it, all the while looking over her shoulder, terrified that Sin would reappear and once more exert that devastating power over her. Finally she gave up, grabbing her duffel bag and purse and running from the small yacht without a backward glance, racing along the busy docks of St. Alphonse until she reached the street and the safe haven of a taxi. She leaned back, her breath coming in sobbing rasps, as she sped her way to the airport. She could always send him the damned ring.

Two hours later she was on a flight to New York. She had taken the first available plane, determined to put the island and her so-called husband behind her as quickly as she could. A night at the airport hotel provided little solace. She could wash the sand, suntan oil and the scent of Sinclair MacDonald from her body. But she couldn't wash away the feel of his hands on her, the way his long, lean body claimed hers with such deliberate lingering. Sleep had eluded her, and she was on her way by seven that morning, taking the air shuttle back to Washington and a taxi to her apartment in Georgetown.

But instead of the haven she expected, she stared at the walls in mutinous hatred. Without a conscious decision she emptied her duffel bag of the warm-weather clothes, filling it haphazardly with sweaters, jeans, and turtlenecks. Every warm pair of socks she owned ended in the bag, along with a stack of novels and her seldom used paints. She had only one duty to perform, and then she'd be free. She stopped for a moment at her bank, and then was off, speeding in her little red Honda Civic down the cool autumn highways to her father's estate.

For once none of her siblings was in sight.

There was no Georgia sweeping down the stairs to cast disbelieving eyes over her disheveled appearance, no sneering Travis to puncture her with sly innuendos. She left the car directly in front of the wide front steps, prepared for a hasty exit, and made her way directly to her father's study. He greeted her precipitous arrival with a scowl, his heavy white brows drawn together.

"It's about time," he snapped. "I've sent Travis out looking for you. Why in hell didn't you call? When did you get in?"

"Last night," she said shortly, throwing herself down on the leather love seat.

His frown deepened. "That's it? Two words? No kiss? No, 'Hello, Pops, I've missed you'?"

She eyed him with deceptive calm. "No. Not until you explain what you thought you were doing, siccing Sin MacDonald on me. Why couldn't you have told me what Greg was trying to do? I certainly wouldn't have defended him."

"How was I to know that?" he countered, moving around the front of his mahogany desk. "You'd been pretty well hooked on him, not to mention putting up with his ... peculiarities willingly enough." A look of distaste shadowed his aristocratic face.

Cathy's heart stopped for a moment, then thudded, her face flushing. "Who told you?" she gasped. "Oh, why should I bother asking?" she added bitterly. "Your hired stooge must have provided you with all the intimate details of my past relationships. After all, you were paying him to spy on me, among other things." For some reason she had thought she couldn't hurt anymore, but the thought of Sin spilling her confidences in her father's disdainful ear was still a further twist of the knife that skewered her heart.

"As a matter of fact, it was Danville who bragged about it," her father said heavily. "Just to convince me how much power he had over you." He moved closer, sitting down beside her and taking her limp, unresisting hand in his blue-veined one. "Listen, honey, I was just trying to protect you. Sin MacDonald is the best in the business—I thought I could count on him to distract you and keep you out of Danville's way. I had no idea he'd go overboard like that. I would have thought arranging to share your hotel room would have been enough."

Another blow to Cathy's solar plexus. "You mean that was part of the whole entrapment?" she demanded.

"Sin's a real professional. Of course he arranged it. And if he felt he had to marry you to do his job, then he'd do it. Trust Sin to be thorough."

"I thought it wasn't a real marriage," Cathy said in a small voice.

"Apparently it is, according to Sin. I can't imagine why, unless he thought you'd see through a phony one. Not to worry, though. My lawyers can dissolve it in forty-eight hours or less. I'll have Harris come over this evening with the papers...."

"I won't be here." She rose abruptly.

"What do you mean, you won't be here?" her father echoed uneasily. "Of course you will. Meg and Charles are coming for supper. She's afraid you might be mad at her. I told her no such thing, but I don't think she'll believe it till you tell her yourself."

"Is she really pregnant?" Cathy snapped, striding to the window and looking out at the winding drive, the neatly landscaped lawns. "Or was that all part of your master plan?"

"Of course she's pregnant! What kind of Machiavelli do you think I am?" he demanded, affronted.

"I really don't know. All I do know is that I'm not staying." She turned back to face him, and her face was bleak beneath the honey gold of her newly acquired tan. "I'm going away for a while. Where no one can find me, or bother me. I would suggest you don't try to find me, Pops. I wouldn't take kindly to another Sin MacDonald showing up at my doorstep."

"But—but what about your annulment?" he protested. "You'll need to sign the papers if we're going to get moving on it."

"Let Sin file for the annulment," she said bitterly. "After all, with the nice little bonus you're going to give him he can well afford it."

"Cathy, Cathy, I don't know what's gotten into

you, girl," her father sighed. "I was only looking out for your interests."

"I'm sure you were, Pops," she said steadily. "But right now it's time for me to take care of myself. I'll call you." Without another word she turned her back on him and left the house, ignoring his angry calls. She passed Travis's Peugeot on the winding drive, ignoring his look of surprise, her face determinedly forward. And she refused to look back until she reached Vermont.

The next six weeks were long, pain-filled ones. As she burrowed into the tiny log cabin halfway up a mountain, she reveled at first in her isolation. None of her family would ever stop to think of Alice, her old college roommate, much less remember that she owned a house and twenty acres in Vermont. She was safe to enjoy herself in her solitude. She read every book in the tiny house, then began making periodic forays to the two-room library in town to stock up on mysteries, romances, biographies, and thrillers. Deliberately she kept all thought of Sin MacDonald from her mind, even when her eyes happened to glance down at the thin gold band that still adorned her finger. It came off easily enough now. Cathy had lost weight, her figure taking on a more willowy look, but for some reason she kept the gold band firmly in place. It was when she found that she wasn't pregnant that she began to realize why.

Of course she hadn't wanted to be pregnant,

she told herself sternly. Not under those circumstances. She had thought it through very calmly when she realized there was a possibility. She would have an abortion. After all, everyone did nowadays. And what kind of life would the poor baby have, born to a father who manipulated women and a mother who was hopelessly in love? ...

That was the key to the matter, Cathy realized, curled up on the couch, her slender fingers wrapped around a cup of coffee. A mother hopelessly in love. Although not a mother this time. And probably never would be. At least, not to Sin MacDonald's children. And instead of relief she felt an aching emptiness.

She should write him, she thought for the twentieth time. Send him his damned ring, and inquire politely if he'd gotten the annulment. After all, she should find out whether she was still a married woman or not. Not that it mattered. In the tiny village of Appleton the only single man was eighty-four and stone deaf. She was hardly besieged by eligible admirers.

But days and weeks passed, and the ring stayed firmly on her finger, and the letter remained unwritten. Until finally, on impulse, as the steep hills were covered with a fresh dusting of snow, she drove into town and placed a long-distance call to Meg.

"Hello?" Meg's somewhat breathless voice came over the line, and Cathy realized with a shock that she hadn't seen her sister since her wedding day.

"Hi, Meggie," she said softly.

There was a long silence on the other end of the line. "Cathy?" she shrieked joyfully. "Oh, my God, is it really you?"

"It is, indeed," she answered with a laugh, the tension draining from her. "How are you doing? How's Junior coming along?"

"Oh, he's fine. Hanging in there like a trouper. I'm fat as a pig already, but at least the morning sickness has passed. But where in heaven's name are you, Cathy? We've been worried sick. Pops calls me almost every day, asking if I've heard from you."

"Do me a favor? Tell him I'm fine, but don't tell him anything else. I—I'd rather keep away from him and the family for a while longer."

There was a long pause on the other end of the line. "It still hurts, does it?" she asked quietly.

"Only when I laugh," replied Cathy grimly. "So tell me, what's the news? How's Pops doing?"

"Pops is just fine, but madder than a wet hen at you for running out. Charles is in seventh heaven, preparing for fatherhood, and Georgia is being as meddling as ever." She paused deliberately. "Oh, and you'll want to hear the latest on your exlover."

Cathy's heart lurched to a stop. "Not really. I couldn't care less about Sin MacDonald."

"I wasn't talking about Sin. I mean Greg Danville. He's in jail, you know."

"In jail?" She was only vaguely interested. "Why?"

"He was brought up on assault charges. Apparently he beat up a young lady who just happened to be a senator's daughter. I gather he doesn't even want to be bailed out. But then, who can blame him after what happened?" There was another suggestive pause.

"All right, Meg, I'll bite. What happened?" Cathy asked wearily.

"Well, just before Greg was picked up he got into a barroom brawl. Apparently he was just sitting in a bar in Georgetown, minding his own business, when this real tall guy came in and picked a fight with him. Broke his nose in three places. The guy sounded a lot like Sin."

Cathy's hand flew to her own nose, touching it gingerly as she remembered her flight from the French restaurant and Sin. "How interesting," she managed in her chilliest voice.

Another pause. "Cathy," Meg said finally, her husky voice earnest, "Sin's in terrible shape."

"Why? Did Greg hit him back? I wouldn't have thought he'd do much damage to anyone Sin's size," she said coldly.

"Don't be deliberately obtuse. Sin's in love with you. He's been going crazy trying to find you this last month, and all his leads have turned up blank."

"Well, he'll just have to try harder. I'm sure Pops is paying him enough to make it worth his while." Cathy's voice was bitter.

"Pops isn't paying him anything. He quit. Over the phone from that island, as a matter of fact. Didn't he tell you?"

"No. Neither did Pops. Not that it makes any difference," she said staunchly. But it did.

"Don't you care about him at all, Cathy? You never used to be so hard-headed. The man loves you."

"What makes you think that? He never told me a word about it," she shot back, amazed to find her hands were trembling. She hadn't known it was that cold.

"Of course he didn't. How could he tell you he loved you when he had to keep lying to you? He was trying to protect you, Cathy. He deserves something better from you than a complete disappearance. You owe him a hearing at least."

"I owe him nothing." She rubbed her hands together to get rid of the chill. "And where did you come up with all this?"

"Sin and Charles really are old friends. They were at Harvard together. Sin's confided in Charles, and Charles has told me—"

"With strict orders to pass it on. Well, no thanks," Cathy finished for her. "He can find some other poor fool and marry her. There are people with more money than us."

"One of whom is Sin!" Meg snapped, her sympathy coming to an abrupt end. "He's George Farwell's nephew, Cath. He doesn't need our money."

"Oh." Another part of Cathy's rage bit the dust. "Well, this is costing us a small fortune. I'll call some time later. Maybe on the weekend."

"How far away are you? When are you coming back?" Meg demanded. "Can I tell Sin you called?"

"No, to the last. I don't know when I'm coming back, and I am not about to tell you where I am. Next thing I know Sin or someone equally unwelcome will show up to drag me back to dear old daddy. I'll be in touch." She hesitated, then finally asked the question that had plagued her mind. "Oh, Meg, you wouldn't happen to know whether Sin has filed for an annulment yet, would you?"

There was a disgusted snort from the other end. "Of course I know. He's done no such thing. You're still legally married. I told you, the man loves you!"

"Oh," she said blankly. And then hung up without another word. She stayed there in the cold Vermont wind, staring at the silent telephone for a full five minutes, lost in thought. Could she risk it again? Did she dare to take one last chance, on the remote possibility that Meg was right, and Sinclair MacDonald *had* fallen in love with her? Or would she spend the rest of her life running and hiding, always tied to a man she hadn't had the courage to face?

It didn't take her long to decide—the ten minutes it took to drive back up the hill to her cabin were sufficient. If Mohammed wasn't a good enough private investigator to find the mountain, then the mountain would have to travel back to Georgetown.

It took her longer than she would have expected to close up the cabin. First she had to arrange to have the water drained and the electricity turned off. The food had to be eaten up or tossed out, the house scrubbed from top to bottom to keep the winter creatures from making an unwelcome home there, to chew through mattresses and get stuck in the fieldstone chimney. Library books had to be returned, the car checked for its twelve-hour trip back to Washington. She checked off each item on the list, staring at it with a look of exhausted satisfaction. She was finally ready. In her purse was Sin's duplicate set of keys, the set that he'd tossed her on their wedding day with great casualness. The keys to the yacht, their hotel room, his BMW. And the keys to his apartment in Alexandria.

In the past few weeks she had staunchly ignored the ramifications of that casual gift, deciding several times that she would toss them out. After all, she would never have a use for them. But something had stopped her—perhaps an unconscious echo of medieval times, when the mistress of the castle was ceremoniously presented with the keys as a symbol of her rank. If Sin had expected their relationship to be a temporary delaying tactic in the Caribbean, why had he given her his Washington keys?

As she started on the first leg of her long journey, she glanced at her reflection in the car mirror. There was a light in her green eyes, a sense of purpose to her soft mouth. Some things were worth taking a chance on, worth fighting for, she thought, putting the car in gear and starting down the winding dirt road. And Sin MacDonald was, despite her earlier misgivings, one of those things.

Chapter Twenty-one

There was no sign of his forest-green BMW in the parking lot adjacent to his building, or on any of the streets around. Hedging her bets, Cathy parked several blocks away, walking the distance through the autumn-cool streets of Alexandria in jeans, high-laced boots and a thick pullover. Compared to Vermont's early winter the weather was positively tepid, and her hips swung with a casual sway as she strolled down the sidewalks. It was nearly evening; almost seven o'clock, and Cathy had been driving for thirteen hours. Thirteen hours that had seen her grow progressively more light-hearted as she neared the Washington area, despite the uncertainty of her reception. When she reached the outskirts of Alexandria she had hesitated, longing for a hot shower and a nap more than anything. But a belated uncertainty crept in, and she knew if she put it off she might never have the courage to beard the panther in his den. He would simply have to take her, travel-stained and exhausted, as she was. She only hoped he'd take her.

There was no answer to her ringing of the red-painted, paneled door of his apartment. By the looks of things Meg had been right — Sin didn't need her money. The understated charm of the building and the foyer proclaimed discreetly that here resided people of wealth and taste. Fumbling with the keys, she tried one after the other, going through the entire set twice before managing to turn the bolt. And then she slipped into the darkened flat, closing the door behind her.

It had a musty, closed-up smell about it, she realized as she moved around switching on lights. She opened a window to air it out, then turned to survey Sin's living quarters.

They suited him, she decided after a long perusal. Leather couches, brass lamps, ancient oriental carpets on the polished hardwood floors. The striking modern painting above the fireplace boasted a signature well-known to Cathy, and the impressionist print in the hallway turned out to be quite real. The burgundy red of the curtains complemented the deep hues of the carpet, and the wood shone with loving care. The place looked like Sin — casual, elegant, and comfortable. And very handsome, she added gloomily, wandering through the beautifully organized country-style kitchen with its gleaming copper and butcher block counters. But she was unprepared for the sybaritic luxury of the bedroom and bath. The kingsize bed dominated the large room, the striking charcoal nudes that hung on the walls adding a touch of sensuality. Those would have to go, Cathy decided impishly. They were far more full-figured than she was—positively Rubenesque, when it came right down to it. She didn't want Sin to have the chance to make odious comparisons.

Sudden doubt assailed her. What if he wasn't glad to see her? What if Meg had read only what she wanted to read into Sin's actions? What if he was glad to be rid of her, and finding her in his apartment was the last thing he wanted?

At that moment her eyes dropped to the bedside table. There was a picture there, a snapshot of a beautiful woman in a bikini. A jealous misery washed over her, and then she stared more closely at the photo. It was a very happy Cathy. Sometime during those four days on St. Alphonse Meg had taken her picture, and Sin had wheedled it out of her. It was in a heavy silver frame, her green eyes laughing up from behind the curtain of blond hair. There was a question in her eyes, a look of doubt that told Cathy that Sin had taken it after all. The day they left their tiny island and headed for disillusionment on Martin's Head. If she looked closely she fancied she could see the hurt lingering, waiting to attack. Carefully she placed the frame back on the table. And then she noticed, lying unobtrusively beside it, the gold chain.

Tears of relief flooded her eyes as the last of her doubts vanished. He wanted her. For the first time in six weeks she found she was hungry. There was scarcely anything in Sin's refrigerator. Finally making do with a cheese sandwich and one of Sin's imported beers, she strolled over to his desk. Pieces of paper littered the top, covered with Sin's bold scrawl. Her name, over and over again. A list of her best friends, complete with addresses and phone numbers, all crossed out. A listing of her car model and license plate. And various other notes concerning her habits, her friends, her favorite pastimes and restaurants. Cathy stared down at them with a wistful smile. For all his legendary proficiency he hadn't been able to find her. She'd covered her tracks a bit too well. A yawn overtook her, and then another, and she rubbed her gritty eyes wearily.

Where was he? If he didn't show up soon she'd be sound asleep, and she had grave doubts about her ability to reenact Goldilocks and the Three Bears. Maybe a shower would wake her up. If Sin came home in the middle of it, well . . . Things would simply have to resolve themselves naturally.

But the hot shower had the opposite effect. Once she stepped from the steaming stall she was barely able to keep her eyes open. Toweling her hair dry, she stepped nude into his bedroom, her toes reveling in the thick brown carpet. He'd had the chain repaired, she noticed. It hung a little more loosely around her slender waist than it had six weeks before, but at least it didn't slide off once she did the clasp.

It had been a fitting gift, she mused. For despite her hurt and betrayal, she was chained to him as surely as if she were manacled. But it was her own overwhelming love that chained her, and therein lay her power and her salvation.

There was a floor-length hooded velour wrapper behind the bathroom door. She pulled it on, and then, on impulse, moved through the apartment, turning off the lights, closing the window, effectively wiping out any trace of her early arrival. And then, switching off the bedroom light, she climbed into his huge bed, chuckling to herself, "And who's been sleeping in my bed?" And then, moments after her still damp head hit the soft feather pillow, she was sound asleep.

The voices woke her from a deep, dreamless sleep. For a moment she panicked, forgetting in the darkened interior of the bedroom exactly where she was. And then, as she returned to full cognizance, the panic deepened. That was a woman's voice out there, a light, sultry female that provided a perfect counterpoint to Sin's deep tones. *Oh, my God,* Cathy thought, the full horror of the situation washing over her. *He's brought a woman home with him.*

Silently she crawled out of the bed, pulling the velour wrapper about her as she tiptoed to the half-opened door and pressed her ear against it, straining to hear their conversation.

"Get some sleep, Sin darling," the woman said companionably, and Cathy gnashed her teeth.

"You look like hell. You've been working too hard, you know."

"I haven't been sleeping well, Barb," he confessed. Cathy could imagine him running a hand through his rumpled brown curls as he made that admission, and her stomach knotted with sudden longing. How was she going to escape before he brought that—that creature into the bedroom?

"Is she worth it, Sin?" the woman's voice came again, and Cathy pressed closer, wondering if she heard correctly.

"Yes." The answer was unequivocal. To Cathy's mingled relief and consternation he put a hand behind the lady's slender back and guided her to the front door. "Tell Frank I appreciate him letting me borrow his best girl for the evening. I don't think I could have managed to remember all that without your taking notes."

"What else is a secretary for? Besides, if Frank can't trust his brother who can he trust? I'm sure you'd do the same for him." She let out a small trill of laughter. "Not that I'm as understanding. I wouldn't care for Frank to spend an evening alone with your Cathy. She's far too pretty, if that picture is any proof." She reached up and gave Sin a sisterly kiss on the cheek. "Find her, Sin. Find her, or get over her."

"I'm trying, Barb," he said morosely. "I've got to." The light in the hall illuminated his face for a moment as he let Barb out, and Cathy drew an involuntary breath of surprise. He looked drawn and haggard, and she could easily believe he hadn't been sleeping well. Was she the cause of that? She could only hope so. Dropping the robe on the thick carpet, she scrambled back into the bed, pulling the covers up to her chin, and prepared to wait.

She didn't have long. First the chink of ice and the sound of a drink being poured filtered in from the living room. Then the sound of his boots dropping on the floor, the muted notes of a bluesy ballad from the stereo. The lights flickered off, the bedroom door opened, and Sin stood there, framed in the doorway, his shirt unbuttoned and pulled from his pants. There was enough light from the streetlamps outside to illuminate the room, casting the bed's lone occupant in the shadows. Without bothering to turn on the light, he kicked the door shut behind him, shrugged out of his shirt, and took a long pull from his drink. And then he stepped on the hastily discarded bathrobe.

"What the hell?" he muttered, scooping it up from the floor. Faint traces of her scent still clung to it, flowering the air. He was suddenly very still.

It was now or never, Cathy thought, her heart pounding against the thin cotton sheet. What could she say? Something cute, light, and clever? Something witty and sophisticated, to set the tone, keep it casual? Slowly she sat up, searching for the right words. And it came out, one perfect word, in a tone of such longing that time seemed to stand still.

"Sin?" Her voice trembled and broke on the word. And then his arms were around her, his lips covering hers, and all that existed in the world were their bodies and their need and love.

No more words were needed. Slowly, achingly, they brought each other to the point of ecstasy and beyond, instinctively knowing what the other needed, answering that need and glorying in their ability to do so. Their union was made all the sweeter by the six week abstinence and the uncertainties, uncertainties that at that moment no longer needed explaining. And as the final moments of passion approached and peaked, Cathy knew that nothing short of force could remove her from her lover's side. As his cry echoed in the night, she knew he felt the same, and together they traveled over the edge of the mountain to dash into a thousand stars against the rocks below.

It was a long, long time before he spoke. Their bodies were drenched with sweat, still warm with the glow of their perfect love. He cradled her body against his, one hand cupping her cheek, his thumb gently caressing her swollen lips as if he couldn't quite believe she was really there. "Don't you ever," he said, and his breathing was still ragged, "leave me again. I don't think I could stand it."

She snuggled closer against his commanding length, a mischievous grin playing about her mouth. "I guess I'd better not. I waited long enough for you to find me, then had to give up and come to you. How you ever got to be so successful as a private investigator is beyond me. Can't find a simple thing like a wife when you set your mind to it," she mocked lightly, giving herself up to the sweet punishment of his kiss at her lack of respect.

"I would think," he said after a long, breathless moment, "that you're more than a match for me. Professionally, and otherwise." There was a longer pause. "I never meant to fall in love with you."

Cathy gloried in the words, even though his body had told her as much over and over again. "I should have warned you," she said sleepily, rubbing her smooth cheek against his chest. "There are times when I never take no for an answer, either."

"Is this one of them?" He cradled her head against his shoulder.

"Anything to do with you is," she replied pertly. His hands reached down and stroked her waist, resting lightly on the gold chain.

"I know why you came back," he drawled. "You just wanted your chain."

"Sin, darling." She raised herself up to look him squarely in the eye. "I didn't need this scrap of gold to feel chained to you." Her face was shining with love. "You still haven't let me say it, you know."

His eyes were very serious as they looked down into hers. "I couldn't, Cathy. I couldn't tell you I loved you when I was busy tricking you, and I couldn't let you tell me. I figured that was the only dignity I could save you.''

A small smile curved her mouth. ''And do I still need a shred of dignity?'' she questioned airily.

His smile met hers. ''No, my love. You have a natural dignity that nothing can take away.''

''Then,'' she said, levering herself above him and resting her hands on his hard chest, ''I love you, I love you, I love you, I love you ...'' She continued it like a litany as her greedy mouth showered kisses on his mouth, his neck, his chest. ''I love you, I love you, I love you ...'' Until his hungry mouth captured hers once more, and there was no longer any need for words.

Chapter Twenty-two

The *Tamlyn* rocked gently beneath her unsteady feet, and Cathy squinted up through the bright tropical sunlight to her husband's amused face.

"Thank heavens you found a more tranquil place to anchor," she said with heartfelt gratitude, the green tinge beginning to leave her face. "I'm not sure if this was the best possible way to spend our first anniversary."

"You've never been seasick before," Sin said lazily, leaning back against the cushions on the deck.

"I've never been four months pregnant before," she replied, the pleased grin that touched her face whenever she thought of it taking the sting out of her words. "And now that we're relatively motionless I'll do just fine. Where exactly are we?" She peered out at the small, secluded cove with dawning, delighted recognition.

"Five hours south of St. Alphonse." He caught her exuberant body with expert ease, laughing tenderly at her. "I told you I could find it again."

"I should have trusted you," she said ruefully, her green eyes shining up at him as she settled herself into the curve of his arm.

"Yes, you should have," he returned lightly, his lips brushing hers. "But I forgive you."

A small chuckle escaped her. "Magnanimous of you. Do you suppose Alexander is going to enjoy having a new cousin?"

"I expect Meg will have them playing together in the cradle. Are you going to dote on ours as much as Meg moons over Alexander?"

"Probably worse." She cast a belatedly worried glance up at his suntanned profile. "Will you be jealous?"

"You forget, I know you pretty well by this time. I have no doubt you have enough for the both of us, and more besides."

With a sigh of complete happiness she pressed closer against his lean, sun-warmed body. "You're absolutely right. And absolutely wonderful."

"Of course I am. And to prove my devotion I'll tell you now that I'd rather sail down to the Caribbean with you vomiting all the way, than with your brother-in-law anytime."

"Charles's snoring being worse than nausea?" she queried impishly. "You're so romantic I don't know how I stand it."

In light punishment his face covered hers, blocking out the bright sunlight as his mouth caught hers in a long, slow, deep kiss. When he finally released her, her heart was pounding, her pulses racing, and the light that shone in her large green eyes was both dazzling and dazzled.

"Not romantic, am I?" Sin grumbled. "I've got a mind not to give you your anniversary present."

"But you already did!" Cathy protested. "This trip—"

"Is ephemeral. In a while it will only be a memory. I wanted something more lasting." He drew a small velvet box from the pocket of his khaki shorts.

"Oh, Sin, I didn't get you anything. . . ." She took the box reluctantly, but he silenced her with one large, warm hand spread tenderly over her rounded belly that swelled gently over the skimpy bikini.

"Hush, love," he murmured. "You've already given me the two most important things in my life."

With trembling fingers she opened the box. There, nestled against the soft velvet, was a long gold chain, with a heart-shaped emerald pendant attached. "Oh, Sin," she whispered.

"You've almost outgrown the other one," he said lightly, his fingers playing with the gold chain that now fit quite snugly around her thickening waist. "So I thought I'd better get you one for your neck. I wanted to make sure you'd always have something to remind you."

She smiled up at him tremulously, her emerald-green eyes bright with unshed tears. "Remind me of how much I love you, how much I'm chained to you? I don't need to be reminded, Sin.''

He shook his head. "No, darling. It's to remind you how much *I* love *you*. And that I'm chained to you just as you are to me, by chains of love as fine and strong as the gold around your waist. Never doubt it, Cathy. Never doubt me.''

It was a plea, not a command, and her answer was in her eyes, in her heart, in her mouth as she kissed him, her softly rounded body pressed against his lean strength. Passion, never far away, flared between them. As Sin scooped her up in his strong arms and started toward the cabin Cathy let out a soft laugh of pure pleasure.

"I think I'm going to enjoy this honeymoon even better than the first one," she murmured as with great dexterity he maneuvered them down into the main cabin and back toward the bedroom.

"And why is that?" he queried, one eyebrow raised.

"Because this time I won't make you wear those ridiculous jockey shorts," she laughed. And reaching around his shoulder, she pushed the bedroom door shut behind them.

Harlequin reaches
into the hearts and minds
of women across America
to bring you

Harlequin
American Romance™

Get this book FREE!

Mail to:
Harlequin Reader Service
In the U.S.
2504 West Southern Avenue
Tempe, AZ 85282

In Canada
649 Ontario Street
Stratford, Ontario N5A 6W2

YES! I want to be one of the first to discover **Harlequin American Romance.** Send me FREE and without obligation *Twice in a Lifetime.* If you do not hear from me after I have examined my FREE book, please send me the 4 new **Harlequin American Romances** each month as soon as they come off the presses. I understand that I will be billed only $2.25 for each book (total $9.00). There are no shipping or handling charges. There is no minimum number of books that I have to purchase. In fact, I may cancel this arrangement at any time. *Twice in a Lifetime* is mine to keep as a FREE gift, even if I do not buy any additional books.

Name _____ (please print)

Address _____ Apt. no. _____

City _____ State/Prov. _____ Zip/Postal Code _____

Signature (If under 18, parent or guardian must sign.)

This offer is limited to one order per household and not valid to current Harlequin American Romance subscribers. We reserve the right to exercise discretion in granting membership. If price changes are necessary, you will be notified.
Offer Expires May 31, 1984.

154-BPA-NAJP

AR-SUB-300

Take these
4 best-selling novels
FREE

Yes! Four sophisticated, contemporary love stories by four world-famous authors of romance FREE, as your introduction to the Harlequin Presents subscription plan. Thrill to **Anne Mather**'s passionate story BORN OUT OF LOVE, set in the Caribbean.... Travel to darkest Africa in **Violet Winspear**'s TIME OF THE TEMPTRESS....Let **Charlotte Lamb** take you to the fascinating world of London's Fleet Street in MAN'S WORLD ....Discover beautiful Greece in **Sally Wentworth**'s moving romance SAY HELLO TO YESTERDAY.

Harlequin Presents...   *The very finest in romance fiction*

Join the millions of avid Harlequin readers all over the world who delight in the magic of a really exciting novel. EIGHT great NEW titles published EACH MONTH! Each month you will get to know exciting, interesting, true-to-life people .... You'll be swept to distant lands you've dreamed of visiting .... Intrigue, adventure, romance, and the destiny of many lives will thrill you through each Harlequin Presents novel.

Get all the latest books before they're sold out!
As a Harlequin subscriber you actually receive your personal copies of the latest Presents novels immediately after they come off the press, so you're sure of getting all 8 each month.

Cancel your subscription whenever you wish!
You don't have to buy any minimum number of books. Whenever you decide to stop your subscription just let us know and we'll cancel all further shipments.